"I can't
we ha...

Tony's words hit hard. "But that's *my* life, Tony," she said, trying to maintain control. "And I'd be bored out of my mind buried away on some isolated island forever."

"Maybe you wouldn't get so bored if you thought about someone besides yourself, and your silly parties and idle chatter."

"That's not fair. I came to Kauai because of you!"

Tony gazed at her for a long moment. "Maybe that was a mistake."

An icy chill gripped her heart. She wanted desperately to hear him say he didn't mean it. She stared at him unable to speak. *I do love him,* she thought, *but I don't really know him anymore.*

ROSEMARY HAMMOND lives on the West Coast but has traveled extensively through the United States, Mexico and Canada with her husband. She loves to write and has been fascinated by the mechanics of fiction ever since her college days. She reads extensively, enjoying everything from Victorian novels to mysteries, spy stories and, of course, romances.

Books by Rosemary Hammond

HARLEQUIN PRESENTS
802—THE HABIT OF LOVING
859—MALIBU MUSIC
896—LOSER TAKE ALL
985—ALL MY TOMORROWS

HARLEQUIN ROMANCE
2601—FULL CIRCLE
2655—TWO DOZEN RED ROSES
2674—THE SCENT OF HIBISCUS
2817—PLAIN JANE

Don't miss any of our special offers. Write to us at the following address for information on our newest releases.

Harlequin Reader Service
901 Fuhrmann Blvd., P.O. Box 1397, Buffalo, NY 14240
Canadian address: P.O. Box 603,
Fort Erie, Ont. L2A 5X3

ROSEMARY HAMMOND

castles in the air

Harlequin Books

TORONTO • NEW YORK • LONDON
AMSTERDAM • PARIS • SYDNEY • HAMBURG
STOCKHOLM • ATHENS • TOKYO • MILAN

Harlequin Presents first edition October 1987
ISBN 0-373-11017-0

Original hardcover edition published in 1987
by Mills & Boon Limited

CHAPTER ONE

THE last strains of 'Auld Lang Syne' drifted away. Outside the Officers' Club, on the lake, a boat tooted its horn, and a siren blared in the distance. There was a sharp crackle of fireworks.

With her arms still locked around Dan's neck, Diana stood in the middle of the crowded dance floor, the noisy crowd surging and shouting around her. Flecks of confetti were scattered in her dark hair, and a long red paper streamer was caught around her bare shoulders. She could hear the popping of champagne corks, the orchestra breaking into a slow dance tune, and she knew she was more than a little tipsy.

She also felt a little reckless. She gazed up at Dan Armstrong through heavy-lidded eyes. The taste of his brief New Year kiss was still on her lips, and she suddenly felt that she wanted more. Pressing herself a little closer up against him, she tightened her hold on his neck and pouted prettily.

'Is that the best you can do, Dan?' she asked in a seductive tone.

The blue eyes shot open, and he held his tall body rigid. Then he smiled, the rather stern features softened, and he firmly reached behind him to pull her arms away.

'I think you're a little drunk, Diana,' he said calmly. 'Either that or you've suddenly become a tease.'

She tossed her dark head so that the thick black hair

hanging to her shoulders swung against her cheeks, and gave him a haughty look.

'Very well,' she said, enunciating her words as clearly as she could. 'Just remember it was your decision.' She took a step backwards and bumped squarely into a couple dancing by. 'Sorry,' she muttered.

She stumbled a little trying to regain her balance, and felt Dan's hands on her arms steadying her. He heaved a sigh, put his arm around her and began to lead her off the dance floor through the crowd.

'I'm going to take you home,' he said sternly.

Her head had begun to hurt, and a slight nausea was threatening to escalate into something really nasty. While Dan retrieved her coat, she walked slowly and carefully through the doors that led to the outside entrance.

It was freezing, a chill December wind—no, January now, she amended—blowing off Lake Washington. She hugged her arms tightly around her body and stood at the railing looking out at the lake, black under the midnight sky, the lights of the boats still out there sparkling against it.

Her head began to clear immediately in the cold night air. She wasn't really drunk, she thought, just a little woozy, and by the time Dan came through the door to wrap her sleek sable protectively around her shoulders, she felt quite sober. The churning sensation in her stomach had settled down, and her headache was gone.

'Are you okay?' Dan asked.

She smiled at him. 'Fine.'

'Shall we go, or do you want to stay?'

Just then a noisy crowd of people came through the door, laughing and stumbling. One of the men was singing loudly off key, and a woman's high-pitched giggle rang out.

'Diana!' she screeched. 'Come with us. We're going on to the Officers' Club at Pier 91. Someone said there was free champagne and supper!'

Diana hesitated. She was tempted. It would be fun, she thought. More dancing, more good times, more drinking. She glanced up at Dan with an enquiring look. He only shrugged his broad shoulders.

'It's up to you. You're the boss.'

Suddenly she felt very tired. The others had gone ahead towards the car park, still shouting to her. 'I guess not,' she called after them. 'I'll see you tomorrow.'

'What's tomorrow?' Dan asked as they started walking slowly down the concrete stairs.

'The party at the Madisons,' she replied, taking his arm. 'They always have a big bash on New Year's Day to watch the Rose Bowl and all those other bowl games.' She waved her free hand vaguely in the air. 'Everyone will be there. Aren't you going?'

He didn't reply until they reached his car. Then he turned and gazed down at her. 'I take it by your question that you have a date already,' he said stiffly.

She shook her head irritably and frowned. 'Oh, Dan, don't be tiresome!' She opened the car door and got inside. 'It's not that kind of affair. Travis Blake is driving me, but you'd hardly call it a date.'

She tucked her long skirt around her legs. Dan closed the door and came around the front of the car to get in beside her. Before he started the engine, he turned and gave her a glance that was half indulgent, half annoyed.

'It looks as though I missed my chance out on the dance floor,' he said with real regret in his voice.

'That's nonsense, Dan,' she said airily. 'You were only being a gentleman.' She smiled at him. 'I count on that from an officer in the United States Navy.'

In the dimness, she could see the hungry look on his face and hear the sharp intake of breath as he watched her. He shoved his key abruptly into the ignition, and started the engine.

'Sometimes I think you *are* a tease,' he muttered as he backed out of the slot. 'You just like leading me on, playing with me.'

'That's not fair, Dan,' she protested. 'I've never led you on. I do apologise for what happened on the dance floor. I had a little more to drink than I'm used to, but you'll have to admit that doesn't happen very often, and I've never done anything like that before, if you want to call it teasing.'

They slowed down at the sentry box near the front gate to the Naval Air Station. A young man in a Shore Patrol uniform glanced briefly at the sticker on the windscreen, stood stiffly to attention and saluted smartly.

'Goodnight, sir,' he said formally.

'Goodnight, sailor,' said Dan. 'And Happy New Year.'

The boy grinned. 'Thank you, sir. Same to you, Commander Armstrong, sir. And to you, too, Mrs Hamilton.'

There was no mistaking the adoring look in his eyes as he grinned at her. Diana flashed him a broad smile and waved. 'Thanks, Johnny,' she called to him. Dan gunned the motor and turned abruptly on to Sand Point Way.

'Good God, Diana,' he grumbled, 'does every man you meet have to fall in love with you?'

'You're very grouchy tonight, Dan,' she said calmly as they headed north towards the Laurelhurst section of Seattle where she lived. 'What's wrong?'

He didn't speak until they'd pulled up in front of her house, just ten minutes later. At the kerb, he switched off the engine, then sat staring blankly ahead for several moments, his hands still gripping the steering-wheel, apparently deep in thought. Finally, he turned to her.

'You must realise by now that I want to marry you, Diana,' he said in a husky voice. 'I've been in love with you for years—you know that. I'm sick of standing in line with all the others waiting for a handout.' He moved slightly closer. 'Say you'll marry me, darling. I do love you. I think you care for me.'

The minute he began his speech, a cold chill clutched at her heart, and she sighed inwardly. It wasn't the first time she'd had to deal with such a situation, but it always made her sad. She did like Dan, and enjoyed his company. He was good-looking, mature, kind, and at thirty-seven, had a brilliant career ahead of him in the Naval Air Force. She would miss him.

She turned to him. 'Dan,' she said softly, 'I told you from the beginning that I didn't want a serious involvement. I never lied to you. Outside of my one lapse tonight on the dance floor, for which I am truly sorry, I've never led you on.'

'That's true,' he admitted gruffly. 'I was out of line to accuse you of it. But you've got to settle down some time, Diana. Why not do it with me?'

Her green eyes widened. 'Why do I have to settle down? There's no law against just having fun, is there?'

'Is that all you want from life, Diana? Just to have fun?'

She shrugged. 'What else is there?'

'What about marriage, a home, children?' He ran a hand over his short blond hair. 'God, even a job! Your whole life is one long round of parties, luncheons, shopping expeditions, teas, bridge clubs. There's more to you than that.'

'Apparently not,' she said lightly. 'I like my life exactly as it is. I don't have to explain it or apologise for it to you or anyone else.' She put her fingers on the door handle and pressed it down. 'Besides, I've already been married.'

He snorted loudly. 'Oh, come now, Diana! You've been a widow for seven or eight years now, and were married for all of six months. You could hardly call that a marriage.'

He was right, of course, she thought, shifting uncomfortably in her seat. She could barely remember what her young husband had looked like. She knew, too, that she used her long widowhood as a protection against serious emotional relationships, as though having been married once somehow absolved her from ever venturing into matrimony again.

In a way, it was even true. In spite of her frivolous reputation and pleasure-seeking lifestyle, she was at rare times aware of a more serious side to her nature. Certainly she had taken her short marriage seriously, and when Tony had been killed, she just knew she would never marry again.

'Surely you can't still be in love with Tony,' Dan was saying now. 'Still grieving over him.'

She laughed. 'Of course not. I was only a girl when I married him, barely twenty, and still was when he died. I don't think about him at all any more. It was all so long ago. I'm a different person now.'

'Are you, Diana? Are you really? Remember, Tony was my friend, too. I knew you both even before you were married, and you were the same then as you are now. You and Tony both, all you cared about was having fun.'

She smiled at him again. 'You still haven't convinced me that there's anything wrong with that, Dan.' She put a hand on his arm. 'Look, you're a serious person, responsible, committed. You want to settle down, have a family. I don't. Neither did Tony, and that's probably why we got along so well.'

'It's also probably why you've hardly given him a thought in all these years, too.'

'Now, that's not fair,' she said, stung. 'I did my share of grieving when he died. But you said it yourself, it was a very short marriage. We were more—oh, playmates, I guess you'd call it, than anything else.'

He put his hand over hers. 'I'm sorry. I didn't mean to criticise you or judge you, and I realise you were only a girl when he died. But now you're a woman, the most beautiful, the most desirable woman I've ever known.' He laughed shortly. 'You've got half the Naval Air Force in love with you, for God's sake.'

'Oh, come on, Dan! No one's really in love with me at all. They just like to take me out because they know I'm not looking for a serious commitment, and also because my father's the Base Commander.'

He gave her hand an impatient squeeze. 'I'm not going to argue the point. All I know is that I'm in love with you, and I want to marry you. Say you'll at least consider it, think about it.'

'No, Dan,' she said without a moment's hesitation. 'I

can't do that. You say you're in love with me, but what you really want is to change me. You want me to be more serious, to make a home for you, probably have your children. I won't do that. Not for any man.'

He frowned and opened his mouth to say something, but she pressed the handle down firmly, pushed the door wide open and got out on to the pavement.

'Goodnight, Dan. Thank you for a lovely evening. And Happy New Year.'

She could feel him watching her as she ran lightly up the front walk on her high-heeled shoes, and it wasn't until she was safely inside, with the front door securely behind her and the lights turned on, that she heard him drive away.

Diana loved her house. It wasn't large, but every detail had been chosen with loving care. Tony's insurance money had left her the money to buy it, and the pension of a Navy pilot killed in the line of duty was more than adequate to meet her needs. Her parents were well off, too, and very generous with their only daughter, who was widowed so young. She'd never had to work, never wanted to, and, thank God, didn't need a second husband to provide for her.

She took off her high-heeled shoes and padded in her stockinged feet across the thickly carpeted living-room, turning lights on as she went and humming a little under her breath. Whenever she came home, day or night, she enjoyed just looking at her house again, each room perfect, each object a reflection of her own taste.

The living-room was done in cheery yellows, pinks and greens, spring colours, chosen to brighten the drab Seattle weather. The carpet, walls and curtains were white, but the delicate floral print of the upholstery and the watercolours hanging on the walls broke the stark monotone cleverly.

As she went up the carpeted staircase to her bedroom, Diana thought over her conversation with Dan, wondering if there were anything she should reproach herself for. She hated hurting anyone. Contented with her pleasant life and cheerful by nature, she liked things to run smoothly, and was a little annoyed at Dan for pressing her tonight over *his* desire to marry.

She flicked on the light in her room, and the rose-shaded lamps cast a warm glow over it. A dainty floral wallpaper covered the walls, the carpeting was a pale grass green, the bedspread and draperies picked up the vibrant colour of the roses in the paper. It was a lovely room, she thought with satisfaction. Every time she came into it, she felt as though she were walking in a garden.

Of course men want to marry, she thought as she hung up her lovely fur, a gift from her parents on her twenty-first birthday. They have all the advantages in marriage. Who wouldn't want a combination maid, valet, cook, nanny, chauffeur and bed-partner just for the price of support? And since two really could live almost as cheaply as one, it cost a man hardly anything to take a wife.

She dropped her diamond earrings on her dressing-table and sat down to remove her make-up. It's the woman who has to pay in marriage, she thought as she creamed her face thoroughly. Look what it costs her! Her freedom, most of all. Her figure, if she has children, and most men seemed inordinately anxious to perpetuate their precious genes in offspring.

She wiped the cream off her face and soaked a cotton pad in astringent lotion to cleanse the residue away.

Then, of course, while he's off at his work or playing golf or drinking with his friends, who's stuck at home with the children?

She started to brush her thick dark hair, one hundred faithful strokes every night, no matter how late she came home. Good looks were maintained by these small disciplines, her mother had preached to her over and over again when she was growing up.

She took off her clothes and hung the dress carefully in the huge cupboard on a pink padded hanger. It was another of her mother's laws that in order to be well dressed, clothes had to be cared for. She stroked the fur, placed the shoes in their proper place on the shelf in the long row of others, and put her discarded underwear in the embroidered satin bag reserved for hand-washing that hung on the cupboard door.

She had nothing to feel guilty about, she decided, as she put on her nightgown and robe. Except for that one silly moment on the dance floor, she'd managed to keep Dan at a distance for years, promising nothing, not by a word, a glance, a gesture.

As she brushed her teeth in the adjoining bathroom, she wondered what in the world had possessed her to come on to Dan like that. He'd given her his usual New Year kiss, just a brief peck on the mouth, actually, when suddenly she'd wanted more than that. She'd been going to New Year parties with him for years, and she herself had limited the extent of the kiss.

It must have been the champagne, she decided finally as she switched off the bathroom light and went back to the bedroom. She'd never felt remotely physically attracted to Dan in the past, or to any other of the numerous young men she'd gone out with through the years. She managed to keep them all at a distance, and had come to believe sincerely that she must be frigid. This didn't disturb her. It seemed to her that sex was highly overrated, a rather messy, sweaty business, as her mother had put it with a sniff, that a woman simply had to put up with.

Had she been cold in her marriage? She could hardly remember. It was so long ago. She'd heard that a person's body changes completely every seven years, that every cell in the body is replaced in that time, and she thought this must be true of the mind, too. She tried to put herself back in the mind of the girl she'd been before her marriage and the wife during those short six months, but it was as though a powerful mental block rose up before her eyes to prevent such a journey into the past.

It doesn't really matter, she thought, as she got into bed. Today is all that counts. When she reached out to turn off the bedside lamp, she realised that she wasn't sleepy in the least. She debated going downstairs to find something to eat, but long habit stopped her.

'If you want to keep your figure,' her mother's voice rang in her ears, 'you must never, ever, eat in between meals.'

With a sigh of regret, Diana reached for the remote control switch and turned on the television set. Perhaps one of the late-night shows would put her to sleep. She flicked the buttons from station to station. All that seemed to be on were old movies, Westerns, mostly, which she detested.

Finally she decided on one of the talk shows and settled back on the pillows to watch the famous host banter back and forth with a well-known pop singer and a midget actress. It was so boring, she thought, she'd be asleep in five minutes.

She was, in fact, just drifting off seconds later, when a loud voice broke into the commercial. 'We interrupt this programme to bring you a special news bulletin.'

Her attention aroused, Diana opened her eyes drowsily to see the face of a familiar newscaster filling the screen, and in the next moment she heard his voice.

'We have just recieved word here in Washington that Anthony Hamilton, the Navy pilot who was shot down behind the Iron Curtain seven years ago, has just been released.'

Anthony Hamilton! She shot bolt upright in bed. That was Tony! She turned up the volume and sat stunned, staring at the screen. The newscaster's voice was still speaking in the background, but the picture had changed to show a tall, gaunt man in an ill-fitting shabby suit walking towards the camera. He was flanked on either side by grim-looking men wearing dark suits and hats pulled down over their eyes. Each of them gripped an arm of the man between them, as though guiding and supporting him at the same time.

'As you will recall,' the voice of the newscaster continued, 'Lieutenant Hamilton was shot down on what the Navy called a "routine training mission" when he had strayed "inadvertently" over Communist territory in Eastern Europe. Speculation at the time, of course, was that he was actually on a reconnaissance flight, which, in plain English, means a spy mission. This was denied at the time by Navy officials, and since Lieutenant Hamilton was reported dead, the matter was ultimately dropped.'

The picture on the screen was fuzzy, and the man in

the middle walked with his head down so that Diana couldn't get a good look at his face. He was painfully thin and walked in the shambling, shuffling gait of an old man.

'The picture you see on your screen now,' said the reporter, 'shows Hamilton being escorted out of the American Embassy in West Berlin, where he was brought from the country, unknown at present, where he has been held prisoner for seven years.'

The screen now showed a cluster of reporters with cameras trained on the tall man and microphones thrust up towards his face. There was an incredible racket as they excitedly shouted questions at him, and for one moment before his two guards spirited him into a waiting black automobile, he glanced directly into the camera.

He didn't utter a word, but the look on his face made Diana catch her breath in a sudden painful rush of emotion. His expression was an agonising combination of confusion and sheer suffering. The eyes were curiously blank, the cheeks hollow. There were deep circles under his troubled dark eyes, and his black uncut hair hung lifelessly over his forehead.

Then the three men were inside the car, the camera following it as they drove away. It shifted back to the newscaster, who continued his report.

'The two men you saw with Lieutenant Hamilton were unidentified, but an anonymous source has informed us that they are American agents, either FBI or CIA. Rumour has it that Lieutenant Hamilton will be taken directly to a naval hospital for observation, but the exact location seems to be a well-kept secret. We have no details on why he was released, but our guess is that he was exchanged for one of our own political prisoners. All we can say at this point is, "Welcome home, Lieutenant Hamilton.'"

The reporter's image faded, the talk show resumed, and Diana was left staring blankly into space. She was sitting straight up in bed, every muscle rigid, her mind simply unable to grasp what she had just seen and heard.

Finally, she felt the overpowering impulse to move, to do something. She jumped out of bed and started pacing around the room, wringing her hands and muttering to herself.

'It can't be Tony. It's not possible,' she kept repeating. The man on the screen hadn't looked even remotely familiar. It was a mistake. Tony was dead. She still had the telegram from the Navy tucked away somewhere, the posthumous medal he was awarded, the flag that had covered his empty coffin at the military funeral.

She ran to the cupboard and reached far back on the shelf to take down the box where she had stored a few of his things, his medals, official documents, some photographs. She hadn't looked at them or thought about them since the funeral.

She put the box on the bed and started to paw frantically through its contents. There it was, the yellow envelope that contained the telegram notifying her of his death. 'We regret to inform you . . .' It hadn't been as cold as that, she recalled, not with his hero's status and her father's position as Base Commander.

There had been the telephone call first, she remembered, from his commanding officer, then the personal visit from a government agent who had been kind, but yet very insistent on finding out how much she knew about Tony's mission. All Tony's friends, mostly other

Navy pilots, had rallied around her and disposed of Tony's clothes and personal possessions. All except the contents of the long-forgotten box on the bed.

There was the small black case with his posthumous medal inside, the highest honour the country bestowed on a military hero. A large manila envelope with official documents. A photograph album.

Slowly she took out the album, almost afraid to look, yet curious to compare her husband of seven years ago with the gaunt stranger she had seen on the television screen. The black cover was grimy from disuse and she brushed away the thin layer of dust before she opened it.

The very first picture was a wedding photograph, she in her long white gown and veil, Tony in his sparkling dress whites. They were just coming out of the chapel on the base through the double row of his brother officers with their swords upraised and crossed above the newlyweds.

Her arm was crooked in his, and they were looking at each other, smiling, their eyes meeting. We look so happy, she thought. And we were, she added. She'd almost forgotten. She stared down at the photograph for several long moments, trying futilely to reconstruct that day in her mind. But it was too remote, too long ago. Slowly she turned the page.

The next photograph was one of Tony alone, caught in a pensive moment some time during the reception at the Officers' Club. Diana drew in her breath sharply at the sight of him. She'd forgotten what a beautiful man he was, and how young!

His dark hair was cut short, Navy style, and his face was deeply tanned against the white uniform. The pose was in profile, giving a clear view of his fine straight nose, his firm chin, the long black lashes of his half-closed eyes. He was unsmiling, an unusual expression for the fun-loving man she remembered, and she gazed fixedly down at the mouth.

It was the feature she had loved most about him, she now recalled. It was an unusually mobile mouth, covering strong even white teeth, which normally would be flashing in one of his broad grins. The upper lip was rather thin, the lower one full and sensuous. It was a wide mouth, but well in proportion to his broad, bony jaw.

Suddenly she slammed the album shut. 'No!' she cried aloud. The man on the screen was not her husband. That haggard face, scarred with the marks of suffering, didn't remotely resemble the young man in the photographs. It was a mistake, she told herself. Someone had made a dreadful mistake. People don't change that much in seven years.

The telephone rang shrilly, breaking the stillness of the room, and she jumped at the sound. It rang again. She stared at the instrument on the bedside table, a pale green, chosen to match the carpeting. She didn't want to answer it. But it kept on ringing.

Finally she knew she had to do it. She dragged herself over to the table and picked up the receiver.

'Hello,' she said dully.

'Mrs Hamilton?' came a deep masculine voice. 'Mrs Anthony Hamilton?'

'Yes.'

'This is Captain Arne Jacobson. I was your husband's commanding officer. If you recall . . .'

'Yes,' she said, recognising the name. 'I recall quite well.'

She had the odd sensation that someone else was holding the telephone and listening to this man, that the real Diana was standing off somewhere watching the scene, as though it were only a play or a movie. Or a nightmare. It certainly couldn't be real.

'I wonder if by chance you've seen the news bulletin about your husband on the television?'

'Yes,' she replied curtly. 'I have.'

'I'm very sorry about that,' he said with a sigh. 'We did our best to keep it quiet until he was actually released into our custody and we confirmed that he really was who they claimed he was, but somehow there was a leak in security and the media got hold of it. You understand, we didn't want to notify you until we were certain of his identity.'

Everything in her resisted, but she had to ask. 'You are certain, though? It really is Tony?'

'Oh, yes,' came the firm reply. 'No question about it. The man they released is Tony Hamilton, your husband.'

CHAPTER TWO

THE next day was utter bedlam, a nightmare of people coming and going in and out of Diana's house, most of them strangers.

Her mother and father appeared first on her doorstep at seven o'clock that morning. She was still in her robe, numb and shaken, having only dozed fitfully during the rest of the night. When she opened the door to see her parents standing there, she could tell by her mother's concerned expression that they knew.

'You've heard?' she asked.

'Yes, darling,' her mother said. 'Arne Jacobson called your father just an hour ago. We came as soon as we got dressed.'

Glancing past them, Diana could see a strange car at the kerb, parked just behind her father's sleek Cadillac. Two men got out of the back seat, one with a large camera, the other pulling along a length of heavy black cable. A third man and a woman emerged from the front seat.

'Dad,' Diana said, with a weak flutter of her hand, 'who are those people?'

Her father wheeled around and stared briefly, then turned back to her. 'Reporters,' he said curtly in his clipped military manner. 'You and your mother get inside. I'll deal with them.'

As he turned and started walking down the steps towards the approaching group of people, her mother gripped her firmly by the arm and pulled her through the open door.

'Come on, Diana,' she said. 'Do as your father says.'

She shut the door firmly behind her and guided Diana down the hall to the spotless kitchen.

'Sit down,' she said, motioning her towards the round oak table by the corner windows. 'I'll make some coffee. You look terrible.'

Diana sank obediently down into one of the padded captain's chairs and watched her mother get down the coffee things from the cupboard above the sink. She was a slim woman in early middle age, immaculately groomed as always, even at this hour of the morning, and totally self-possessed. Not a hair was out of place and her careful make-up was flawless.

'Mother,' Diana choked out, 'Tony is alive!'

'I know, dear,' said her mother, rattling china and rummaging in a drawer for silverware. 'Isn't it wonderful? He's a real hero.' She gave Diana a sharp glance over her shoulder. 'After you've had a little breakfast, you'd better get dressed and make yourself presentable. You're going to have to face those reporters eventually. Your father knows how to deal with them, but he can't hold them off for ever.' She smiled brightly, then turned back to set the coffee-pot on the stove. 'You'll be in all the newspapers and on television, and you've got to look your best!'

Diana was on the verge of tears, and she could feel herself moving closer towards the edge of hysteria. She simply couldn't seem to communicate her feelings to her mother.

'Mother!' she cried. 'Tony is alive! Don't you understand what that means?'

'Well, of course I do, Diana,' said her mother, giving her an impatient glance.

'No, Mother,' Diana said, rising out of her chair and leaning forwards, her knuckles resting on the top of the table, 'I don't think you do know what it's doing to me inside. I feel—I feel . . .' Her voice broke off on a sob.

Her mother only gave her a blank uncomprehending stare. Then her eyes softened. She set down the can of coffee and walked over to the table, looking down at her daughter.

'It's the shock, dear,' she said soothingly. 'I do understand. It'll just take you a while to get used to the idea.'

Diana stared at her mother, the green eyes wide and haunted. 'Mother,' she whispered, 'I don't want to get used to the idea.'

Her mother lurched a step backwards as though she'd received a physical blow. 'That's nonsense, Diana! What are you saying? You just aren't thinking straight yet.'

After Captain Jacobson's call, Diana had spent most of the night either pacing or sitting on a chair in her bedroom staring numbly into space and had done nothing else *but* think. She realised that she was still in a state of shock, even now, but she also knew her mother was wrong, that her thinking was quite clear, and her conclusions firm.

'Mother,' she said, calmer now that she had her full attention, 'try to understand. That man on the television screen was not my husband. He's a stranger.'

Her mother stood there, a bewildered look on her face. 'Diana, the Navy doesn't make mistakes like that. If they weren't sure of his identity, they never would have called to inform you of it. They have fingerprints, dental records . . . '

'Oh, it's probably Tony Hamilton all right,' Diana broke in impatiently. 'But it's not my husband. I don't have a husband any more. I hardly ever did, it was so long ago and lasted such a short time.' She could hear her voice rising, feel the panic threatening again, and made herself go still.

'Well, of course,' her mother said briskly, 'it will take some getting used to. It will seem a little strange at first, but after you've gone to see him, spent some time with him . . .'

'Gone to see him?' Diana whispered. 'What do you mean?'

'Didn't Arne tell you when he called?' The coffee had started to perk, and she went back to the stove to turn down the burner.

'Tell me what?' said Diana to her mother's back.

'They're flying you out there right away to be with him.'

'Flying me where?'

Her mother turned around again to face her. 'Why, to Honolulu, of course. He's in the naval hospital at Pearl Harbor. Your father and Arne discussed it this morning on the telephone. They decided that the sooner you leave, the sooner all this publicity will die down.'

Diana could almost palpably feel her lovely life, her safe world, come crashing down around her. It was as though she were being drawn inexorably on a path she had no control over, a path she had no desire to follow, a path that would mean the end of her happiness and security. Everything in her protested against the web she was caught in. Somehow she must make all these people who were calmly deciding her future—her parents, the news media, the Navy—understand that she didn't want to go to Honolulu, didn't want to see him again, didn't want to be married to that gaunt stranger.

Just then the front door opened and closed firmly, and she heard her father's ponderous tread approaching the kitchen. In a few seconds he appeared at the door, a self-satisfied smile on his handsome face.

'There,' he said, brushing his hands off, 'I got rid of them for now.' He eyed his daughter sternly. 'But you're going to have to face them eventually, Diana.' He sniffed the air. 'Coffee smells good,' he said to his wife. He sat down at the table across from Diana. 'Well, my dear, how does it feel to know your husband is still alive? And a hero, at that?'

It feels terrible, she wanted to scream, but long years of habit stopped her. Her father was a rather remote, disciplined man, so used to obedience in his subordinates that the air of command about him carried over even into his family. She simply didn't dare cross him. He would never understand her feelings. Feelings didn't count with her father, only doing one's duty and obeying one's superior officer mattered to him.

'I—I'm not sure yet how it feels,' she replied weakly. 'It's all so confusing. Do you know what happened?'

'Well, he was shot down on that mission seven years ago. It's still hush-hush why he was there and what he was doing over Communist air space.' He shrugged his broad shoulders. 'That's not important now. Apparently he was badly hurt in the crash and has spent the last several years in a prison hospital somewhere in Eastern Europe. Arne Jacobson says he's in pretty bad shape,' he added grimly.

'You mean they mistreated him?' she asked, horrified.

He shrugged again, then accepted a cup of coffee silently from his wife. She set a cup down in front of Diana, then took the chair between them.

'All that will come out in time,' he said between sips of the scalding coffee. 'The important thing now is to put a lid on all this publicity. The Navy wants its heroes, but it's essential that the spy aspect of the story be played down. That's why you've got to go to him as soon as possible.'

'What do you mean, Dad?'

He waved a hand in the air. 'You know—make everything look as normal as possible. His wife rushing to his side, the reconciliation after seven years of believing he was dead.'

Diana was horrified at her father's words. *He's talking about me as though I were a puppet instead of a human being! The Navy jerks the strings, and I dance.* An icy calm began to settle over her. *I just won't do it,* she thought.

'And what if I don't want to go?' she asked quietly.

He shot her a withering glance. 'Don't talk nonsense, Diana,' he said briskly. 'You have to go, whether you want to or not.'

She quailed before the certainty in his tone, the sure ring of authority. Still, she had to give it one last try. 'Dad,' she said in a pleading tone, 'I don't even know this man. How can you ask me to go to him and pretend I'm his wife?'

'I do ask it,' he returned sharply. 'Your country asks it. It's your duty.' His voice softened slightly as if her distress had finally broken through to him. He put a hand on hers, a rare display of affection for him. 'It's only until the publicity dies down, Diana. You may have to pretend for a while. Then, when the furore goes away, you can do what you please about your marriage. Remember, it's been seven long years for Tony, too. He's been through a lot, and certainly he will have changed as much as you have.'

Diana stared blankly at him. She'd never thought of that. In fact, through the whole shocking experience, she hadn't thought of Tony at all. She still couldn't connect in her mind her dimly-recalled young husband and the strange man she'd watched on the television screen. She could still see the lines of suffering in his face, the look of bewilderment and defeat in the lifeless eyes.

Her father was right, she decided at last. Whether she liked it or not, she was caught up in this thing and would have to ride it out to the end. For everybody's sake, her own included, she'd have to go through with this charade, act the part for the news media, and then, when it was over, she could come home, get a quiet divorce, and resume her pleasant life.

She smiled at her father. 'All right, Dad,' she said, 'I'll do it.'

'Good girl,' he said, giving her hand a squeeze. 'Now, you're going to have to talk to the reporters some time today. I only got rid of them by promising them an interview with you later this morning. And Arne Jacobson is sending a man over to brief you about the details of your trip.' He eyed her speculatively. 'You'd better get dressed now. It's going to be a hectic day.'

The telephone rang just then, and her mother went to answer it. From then on, it rang almost constantly, and the nightmare began.

Later that day, Diana sat in the Boeing 747 looking down at the blinking lights of Honolulu, just as dusk was falling. She had left the Seattle airport in a cold wintry drizzle. Now, the dark blue sky was still suffused with a reddish glow from the sun that had just sunk below the horizon, and there was still just enough daylight left to see the towering palms, sandy beaches and pounding surf of Waikiki.

Once she'd realised that all that was really required of her was a good job of acting, her churning emotions had settled down at last, and she'd gone through all the motions, done whatever she was told, just like a docile child who knew that the better it behaved, the sooner the unpleasantness would be over.

She'd sat calmly through the interview with the reporters, both in her own living-room and at the airport, answering all their questions graciously, every inch the loving wife who was overjoyed at her husband's return from the grave.

Her father was by her side throughout the whole ordeal, then later Dan Armstrong had come to give her moral support, and the man from the government, who had briefed her about what lay ahead. He had been polite, but distant, detached, and very businesslike.

His attitude towards her had been exactly that of a commanding officer sending her into battle, issuing clipped orders that he expected her to obey. That was fine, she thought, as the plane circled the Honolulu airport and prepared to land. That was exactly the way she felt.

As the plane taxied along the runway, she began to gather her things together. The government man had told her she would be met at the airport by another agent, then taken to her hotel suite at the Royal Hawaiian. Tomorrow she would be driven to the naval hospital at Pearl Harbor to visit her husband for the first time.

He had also told her to expect to be met by another barrage of reporters, and she was prepared mentally for the ordeal. Having been through it twice now, she knew she could handle it. All she had to do was distance herself, put on a happy smile and act her proper part, just as though she were walking on stage in a play.

Still, when she stepped out of the plane and started down the steps that led to the tarmac, the sudden popping of flashbulbs and the shouts of the crowd below took her somewhat aback, and she paused for a moment. Then, out of the crowd, another of those grimly efficient men in dark suits made his way towards her and met her in the middle of the stairs.

'Mrs Hamilton,' he said in a low voice, 'I'm special agent Lindstrom.' He flashed her his identification and took her firmly by the arm. 'I'm going to drive you to your hotel, but first I'm afraid you'll have to speak to the reporters.' He gave her an enquiring look.

She nodded. 'I understand.'

She put on her broadest smile then, and they walked down towards the waiting crowd. At the bottom of the steps, Diana stood quite still clutching her handbag and waiting.

'How does it feel, Mrs Hamilton?' came the voice of a woman reporter who was thrusting a microphone into Diana's face. 'How does it feel to find out your husband is still alive?'

Diana put on her most charming smile, spread her arms wide and gazed directly into the woman's avid, inquisitive, and curiously cold eyes. Remember, she told herself, I'm only playing a part.

'Well, how would you feel if you were in my shoes?' she asked with a little laugh and passed on.

It was a friendly crowd, and eventually they let her through. When they finally arrived at the waiting car, Mr Lindstrom got in the back with Diana, and the driver, tooting his horn, pulled slowly away from the crowd. Diana leaned her head back and closed her eyes.

Mr Lindstrom briefed her on the way to the hotel. 'You'll be able to take it easy and get some rest tonight,' he said. 'Have dinner in your room, don't answer the telephone. You can have your calls held, if you want. Tomorrow will be a big day. I'll pick you up at ten o'clock and take you to the hospital. I'm afraid you'll have to run the gauntlet of reporters again. They don't know when you're coming and will probably be camped at the gate all night.'

Tomorrow, she thought. Tomorrow I'll see him. She opened her eyes and turned to the man sitting beside her.

'How is he?' she asked. 'Tony?'

The man's eyes glazed over. 'I don't really know. You'll have to discuss that with his doctors. All I know is that he'll be in hospital for several more days. Perhaps weeks,' he added hesitantly.

Weeks! she thought. And what am I supposed to do in the meantime? Aloud she said, 'Will I be staying at the hotel all that time?'

'That's the plan,' he replied. 'Then, when your husband is released from the hospital, we'll have a beach house on Kauai ready for you. The publicity will have died down somewhat by then, and you shouldn't be bothered. He'll need some time to convalesce.'

Diana gave him a sharp, enquiring look, but that was obviously all he was going to say. She'd just have to wait until tomorrow.

Promptly at ten o'clock the next morning, Mr Lindstrom appeared in the lobby to pick her up. She was waiting for him by the desk, anxious to get this ordeal over with. As he had suggested, she'd had her meals sent up to her room to avoid the reporters, but, glancing around the pleasant lobby now, she could see no sign of them.

She'd dressed carefully, however, just in case, in a plain, beautifully cut linen dress of a light green colour that just matched her eyes. She'd slept well the night before, and this morning, as she put on her make-up and combed her hair, she could see that the signs of strain and shock were slowly disappearing from her face. It was as though once she had made up her mind to go through with what was expected of her, she felt more in control of her own destiny.

'Good morning,' said Mr Lindstrom. He nodded briefly. 'Are you all ready to go?'

She wondered if these government agents ever smiled. They all seemed to be cut out of the same pattern, solemn-faced and gimlet-eyed, as though constantly on the look-out for spies lurking even behind the potted palms that dotted the lobby of the hotel. This one was middle-aged and balding, possibly somebody's father, even a doting grandfather, but he still had 'that look' she had come to associate with government agents.

'Have the reporters given up?' she asked as they walked side by side towards the entrance. 'Or has a more sensational story come along?' she added hopefully.

'No such luck, I'm afraid,' he said. He guided her to the car waiting at the kerb out in front of the hotel, and got in the back seat beside her. 'They'll be at the gate of the naval base.' He nodded at the driver, who immediately started the engine. Mr Lindstrom eyed Diana narrowly. 'Think you're up to another interview?'

'I think so,' she replied. 'I'm almost getting used to it by now.'

It was a lovely morning, the sky a sparkling blue, the towering palm trees that seemed to be everywhere almost black against it. The streets of the city were crowded with tourists, most of them dressed in the garish floral shirts and dresses sold on the island, and all of them with either binoculars or cameras slung around their necks. Many of the women still wore their colourful leis, those bright garlands of native orchids and hibiscus that were presented to them on arrival.

Out beyond the wide, shimmering sands of Waikiki stood the bulky mass of Diamond Head, the dormant volcanic crater which protected the beach from storms, and as they drove along, she could see the surfers riding the gigantic waves that pounded incessantly on the shore.

It was only five miles from Honolulu to the naval base at Pearl Harbor, and they drove in silence for most of the way. As they approached the huge installation with its rows of familiar grey buildings, so typical of every naval base she'd ever seen, Diana's pulse rate began to pick up.

She turned to the man beside her. 'Perhaps you could fill me in on the details,' she said nervously. 'I'm not quite sure what to expect.'

'First you'll have to talk to the reporters.' They were

approaching the gate now, and he leaned forward to point out the cluster of people gathered near the sentry box. 'I see they've got their cameras and microphones all set up.' She only nodded.

'Then,' he went on in the familiar monotone, 'you're to meet briefly with Captain Jacobson.'

She shot him a look. 'He's here?'

The man nodded. 'Yes. He flew out from Washington early yesterday. He wants to talk to you before you see your husband.'

'I see.' She only vaguely remembered the man who had been Tony's commanding officer and was an old friend of her father's.

'You'll have a short private visit with your husband after that,' he went on. 'Then you'll have a chance to talk to his doctor. That should bring us up to noon, and I'll take you back to the hotel.'

They stopped outside the tall chain-linked fence that enclosed the entire ten thousand acres of the sprawling base, parking near the gate where a stony-faced sentry patrolled.

Immediately, the swarm of reporters converged on the car. Diana answered all their questions in the familiar platitudes, smiled when they asked her to, and in a few minutes it was over. The gate opened at a nod to the sentry from Mr Lindstrom, and they drove through.

The grounds inside were beautifully kept, with neatly trimmed lawns and the ubiquitous palms. The lovely sheltered harbour itself was clearly visible as they approached the hospital, and several men in uniform were strolling along the spotless pavement.

Inside the cool, quiet hospital, Mr Lindstrom led Diana to a small private office, where a slim, grey-haired man in a captain's khaki uniform was sitting at a bare desk. He rose to his feet smartly as Diana entered and walked towards her with his hands outstretched, a wide grin on his face. She heard the door behind her close quietly as Mr Lindstrom left the room.

'My dear Diana,' the man in uniform said, taking her hands in his. 'You probably don't remember me, but I have a clear memory of you as a little girl in pigtails when your father and I were both stationed at Pensacola.'

'Captain Jacobson,' she said. 'I'm afraid not, but my father has spoken of you often.'

'Let's sit down,' he said, gestering to a leather-covered couch along one wall of the small room. 'Now,' he said, when they were seated side by side, 'I'm sure you're anxious to see Tony, but I thought I'd better fill you in first on his condition.'

'Yes,' she murmured, 'I'd appreciate that.'

He frowned then and looked away from her as though considering his words carefully. 'He's been through a lot,' he said finally, turning back to her. 'He was only released three days ago, and while the doctors say there's every chance for a full recovery, he's very weak, undernourished, and . . .' He broke off and gave her a sharp look. Then he sighed. 'I might as well be frank with you. Your father tells me your character is strong enough to take it.'

Diana clutched at the handbag in her lap, a sudden knot of fear forming at the pit of her stomach. Was Tony crippled? she wondered. Did he have some terrible disease? Would she spend the rest of her life nursing a handicapped husband?

'What is it?' she said finally in a low voice.

'Tony was hurt in the crash, of course,' he went on. 'Some bones broken, burns, a few gashes. But he was young and strong, in top physical condition. It was what happened later that is causing his present problem. You see, he was in prison the whole seven years. They treated him as a political prisoner, a spy.'

'You mean they tried to get information from him?' she asked. He nodded grimly, and then it dawned on her what he was driving at. 'Are you saying they tortured him?' He nodded again, and she closed her eyes, swaying a little as a wave of dizziness passed over her.

'Are you all right?' she heard him ask in a tone of concern.

She opened her eyes and stared at him. 'How bad is it?' she asked tightly.

He shrugged. 'Physically, not that bad. Oh, there are various injuries, some scarring, but nothing that won't heal in time.' He gave her a grave look. 'It's his mental condition they're really concerned about.'

'His mental condition?' she echoed. Good lord, she thought, what have I got myself into? 'You mean, he's insane?'

'Oh, God, no! Nothing like that,' he assured her quickly. 'He's perfectly lucid and rational, just . . .' He stood up. 'Why don't you go and see for yourself? I just wanted to fill you in on the background before you saw him so that you'd be prepared. After your visit, you can talk to his doctor. He can give you a much better picture of his condition than I can.'

Diana rose to her feet, then, and walked with him through the door and down a long, wide corridor. At the end of it, they turned a corner, and at the second door on the right, Captain Jacobson stopped.

'This is his room,' he said. 'I'll leave you now. The doctor has limited his visits to half an hour. I'll come back then.'

He turned and strode off down the corridor, his shoulders squared in a typical military bearing, his tread even on the polished floor, as though marching to the cadence of a drum.

When she was alone in the silent hall, Diana was consumed with a sudden panic. She had to fight down the urge to turn and run, as far away from the drab hospital as possible, back to the hotel. I could just leave, she thought wildly. I'm not a prisoner, after all. I could just tell them—Captain Jacobson, Mr Lindstrom—that I can't go through with it.

I could get on a plane and be back in Seattle, in my own home, by tonight. I could get all this behind me like a bad dream. For one second, she honestly believed she would do just that.

Then she thought of her father, of his stern admonition to her that she must do her duty. How could she face him if she ran away now? And the reporters! She shuddered as she thought of that avid mob, hungry for news of any kind, the more sensational the better. They'd crucify her in the press.

Her shoulders slumped. Much as she hated it, she had to go through with it. She *was* a prisoner, at least for now. But only up to a point. I will not be coerced into anything permanent out of pity, she vowed to herself, nor be tied to a stranger for the rest of my life out of a sense of duty.

She'd have to stay here in Honolulu until Tony was stronger, she decided, but then he'd have to be made to understand her position and release her from a marriage

that had died years ago. And she definitely was not
going off alone with him to the isolated beach house on
Kauai that Mr Lindstrom had mentioned.

There was a small window set in the door to his room,
perhaps a foot square, and before opening the door she
glanced inside. It was a small, typical hospital room,
painted white with one window overlooking a pleasant
garden where pale orchids and red hibiscus bloomed.
Beyond it, the well manicured green lawn stretched
downwards to the sea.

In the narrow metal hospital bed, the figure of a man
was outlined under the neat white blanket. His bare
arms were outside the covers lying quietly at his sides,
and his dark head was turned away from her on the
pillow. He seemed to be asleep.

Diana took a deep breath, turned the handle of the
door and walked inside. The window was open, a soft
balmy breeze blowing in through it, a powerful scent of
flowers heavy on the air. In the distance she could hear
the tramp of feet, a marching cadence, as a troop of men
in uniform paraded by to the crisp barked orders of their
leader. A whistle blew shrilly.

The man in the bed hadn't moved. She closed the door
quietly and went to the foot of the bed. She stood there
silently for some time, studying him.

Although she could see a faint resemblance to the
Tony Hamilton she had married in the dark hair, the
straight nose, the firm chin, the man in the bed could
have been a stranger. His cheeks were painfully
hollowed, his skin pale and unhealthy-looking, as
though he'd been very ill. He was wearing a white
hospital gown, and she could see the sharp ridges of his

collarbone under the low neckline, the thin arms beneath the short sleeves.

Her heart went out to him in a sudden rush of pity. The lines of suffering etched in his gaunt face were horrible to see, and she felt the same tender compassion for him as she might a wounded animal, a hurt child. But nowhere could she find a trace of love.

She didn't know what to do. Should she wake him? She glanced at her watch. She still had twenty-five minutes left before Captain Jacobson would come back. There was a straight chair beside his bed, facing him. Maybe she should just sit there quietly and wait for the time to pass.

She crossed over to the chair and sat down. Tony still hadn't moved, but now she could hear his steady, even breathing and see the rise and fall of his chest under the thin cotton blanket. He was quite a tall man, and his feet reached to the very end of the bed.

As she sat there watching him, a sudden spasm of pain passed over his haggard features and he seemed even more alien to her than he had before. Tony had been a cheerful, good-natured, insouciant young man, always ready to have a good time.

Then he opened his eyes. For a moment, as they met hers, she had a brief intimation of the old Tony in the flash of recognition she saw there. In the next second it was gone, glazed over in a shuttered, closed-in look.

She smiled at him. 'Hello, Tony,' she said. The name sounded strange on her lips as she uttered it. Tony was dead, her inner voice insisted. 'How are you feeling?'

He didn't say anything at all, but the dull eyes narrowed and a deep frown creased his forehead.

Finally he looked away and stared up fixedly at the ceiling.

'What are you doing here?' he said at last in a flat, expressionless tone of voice.

Diana was shaken by the note of hostility in his manner. 'Didn't they tell you I was coming?' she asked hesitantly.

'They told me.'

She stared at him. This wasn't working out at all as she'd expected. She'd had herself all braced for a tearful reconciliation scene, had actually planned ahead for ways to extricate herself from it gently, and now he was acting as though she were an intruder.

She laughed nervously. 'Captain Jacobson made all the arrangements, you know. The Navy apparently thought you were well enough to see me.'

He darted a cold look at her. 'Is that why you came, Diana? Following orders?'

She didn't know what to say. His assessment of her situation was quite accurate, but it seemed terribly crass and unfeeling of him to come right out with it like that.

'I've been watching you on television,' he said, with a nod at the set mounted on the opposite wall. 'You did a marvellous job of acting.' He gazed quizzically at her. 'Perhaps you missed your calling.' A slight smile quirked on his mouth, but his dark brown eyes were cold and distant. 'You're looking quite well, Diana, as beautiful as ever.'

She didn't know how to answer that. He was staring at the ceiling again, and there was another long silence. When he finally spoke again, his voice was hollow, as though speaking from a great distance.

'I want you to leave, Diana,' he said.

She half-rose out of the chair. 'Yes, of course,' she said. 'I don't want to tire you. I don't know when they'll let me come back, but ...'

'No,' he growled. He fixed her with a hard look. 'Don't come back. I want you to leave Honolulu. Go back to Seattle, and don't come here again, ever.'

He turned his head away from her then, and the eyes closed. Diana stood there for a few tense moments, gazing down at him, but he had shut her out completely, and she knew he wouldn't speak to her again.

Slowly, she turned and walked out of the room.

CHAPTER THREE

DON'T you understand?' Diana shouted at the stone-faced Mr Lindstrom two hours later. 'He doesn't want me there!'

They were in the sitting-room of her hotel suite and had been arguing steadily ever since their return from Pearl Harbor. She had started out in a calm, reasonable tone, telling him that perhaps it would be better for her to go back home, at least until Tony was stronger, but had got nowhere.

Mr Lindstrom had never raised his voice, never pleaded, never scolded or threatened. He was simply immovable, like a great pile of boulders, a mountain, she thought, and just kept insisting that in time Tony would accept her visits, probably even come to look forward to them.

Now, with this last outburst, when she had ended by actually stamping her foot in frustration, she was gratified to see a slow look of alarm spread over the man's imperturbable face. She had finally got through to him. He took out a handkerchief, wiped his bald head and sighed deeply.

'He just doesn't want me,' she repeated more calmly. 'I'm not doing any good here. I'm going back to Seattle.'

She went to the window and stood looking out at the beautiful curving white beach, the blue sea. All she wanted was to go home. She'd been willing to go along with the charade for as long as it was necessary. What she hadn't been prepared for was that flat rejection, and it stung more than she cared to admit.

'Listen,' Mr Lindstrom said in a kinder tone from behind her. 'Just stick around for a few weeks, at least until he gets out of the hospital. Make a token appearance every day, and if he won't see you—well, just leave. Go snd see the sights. Sunbathe. Go surfing. At government expense, of course,' he added hastily.

She whirled around and gave him a scathing look. 'Sunbathe?' she asked incredulously. 'Go surfing?'

'Well,' he said limply. 'You could try.'

The expression on his face was so comical that she had to laugh. Oh, well, she thought, what do I have to lose? Her father would be furious if she left now anyway. Why not get a tan, see the sights? She would have done her precious duty, satisfied the reporters and these stern men, then she could go home with a clear conscience and resume her own life.

'Oh, all right,' she said with a sigh. 'Two weeks.'

From then on, Diana's days fell naturally into a pattern that became almost pleasant. She got up when she woke up, had a leisurely breakfast in her room, then showered and dressed. At ten o'clock, Mr Lindstrom would arrive in the car and take her to the hospital, where she would go to the small office and chat for her allotted half-hour with either Captain Jacobson or one of Tony's doctors.

After that first day, she made no further attempt to see Tony; in fact, she deliberately stayed away from that end of the hospital. He didn't want to see her; she wasn't interested in seeing him. She would stay the two weeks, as promised, do her duty, for appearances' sake, then go home.

Even the doctors concurred. Apparently, Tony had made his wishes on the subject quite clear to them, because on the second day one of them had been in the office with Captain Jacobson to greet her when she arrived. He was a slight, mild-mannered man with sandy thinning hair and wore a pair of steel-rimmed glasses that kept slipping down on his short nose.

His name was Dr Phillips, and when Diana entered the office, all prepared to do battle if they tried to force her into barging in on Tony again, he gave her a nervous smile as he shook her hand and immediately broke into profuse apologies.

'I'm so sorry, Mrs Hamilton,' he said, pushing his glasses back up on his nose, 'for the little—um— unpleasantness with Tony yesterday.' He shook his head. 'I'm afraid it was a little too soon for such an emotionally charged meeting.'

'Dr Phillips is Tony's psychiatrist, Diana,' Captain Jacobson explained. He had been hovering nearby, a worried look on his face. 'He feels that when Tony is stronger physically, he'll be more—ah—receptive to your presence.'

'Um, yes,' Dr Phillips agreed, nodding and smiling deferentially. 'He's been through a shocking experience, shocking. Just give him a few more weeks, Mrs Hamilton. He is making progress. We've started him on an intensive physical therapy programme and will soon have him out jogging a little in the sunshine every day. He's already gained back some of his weight and will soon be quite fit physically.'

'Of course,' Diana said calmly. She wasn't going to argue. She'd promised two weeks, and that would be it. Then she could go home.

In the afternoon, she would lie on the beach and swim in the surf for an hour or two, then get dressed again and go shopping or sightseeing. She visited Kapiolani Park at the base of Diamond Head, with its collection of brilliantly coloured tropical birds. She went to Pauli, the thousand-foot-high cliff at the upper end of Nuuanu Valley, with its magnificent view of the entire north eastern coast of the island. She visited the Royal Mausoleum in Honolulu which held the remains of five Hawaiian kings and Hawaii's only reigning queen.

She bought a colourful *muu-muu* on one of her shopping expeditions, a loose cotton gown of brilliant red and white, and wore it to a *luau* at the hotel one evening, a lavish meal of roast pig prepared in an underground *imu*, or oven.

The reporters, sensing that no more interesting stories would be forthcoming from the affair, left her pretty much alone now. She and Tony were yesterday's news. This suited her plans perfectly. Not only did it leave her free to wander around the city at will without a gaggle of newshounds following her around, but when the time came for her to leave, she might be able to slip away quietly. She would start divorce proceedings as soon as she got home, and they could just make of that what they would.

On their daily rides to the hospital, Mr Lindstrom occasionally broached the subject to her of flying over to the island of Kauai, just to take a look at the house where Tony would be sent to convalesce when he was released from the hospital. But she always refused flatly even to discuss it.

Finally, one day in the second week of her stay, Captain Jacobson himself raised the issue with her. They were in the same small office where they usually met while she was supposed to be visiting Tony.

'Mr Lindstrom tells me you refuse to go to the house on Kauai,' he said sternly, standing over her.

They had never discused the future before, and Diana quailed a little under his commanding air. 'I don't really see the point,' she said defensively. 'That man is not my husband, I'm not his wife.' As she spoke, her courage grew. 'Throughout this whole thing, no one has ever bothered to ask me how I felt about it,' she went on. 'First my parents, then the government and the Navy, the reporters, and you yourself have just told me what to do, and I've done it. Now, it's obvious that Tony doesn't want this marriage any more than I do.'

'Tony doesn't know what he wants!' he snapped. 'It's got to be up to you now to make decisions about your future.'

She gazed up at him, still a little cowed by the ring of authority in his voice. Then she thought, it's *my* future, after all, mine and Tony's. They have no right to force us into a situation neither of us wants just to avoid bad publicity for themselves. She stood up and faced him defiantly.

'My mind is made up,' she said quietly. 'I'm leaving at the end of the week. That *is* my decision.'

She could tell he didn't like it, but to her intense surprise, he backed down. He sighed, shook his head, and opened his mouth to argue, but something in the determined lift of her chin must have told him it wouldn't do any good, and he remained silent.

Finally, it was the day of Diana's last visit. She had made her flight reservations for the first plane out tomorrow, and her bags were all packed. She still hadn't told her parents she was coming home or that she intended to divorce Tony, but she decided that if she could face down the formidable Captain Jacobson, she could tackle her father.

Mr Lindstrom came to pick her up as usual, and dropped her off at the hospital. It was a rather strained drive. He'd obviously given up trying to persuade her to stay. He just sat over on his side of the back seat sunk in a morose silence and stared out of the window.

At the hospital, she went straight to the small office where she'd been used to spending her half-hour, and was surprised to see it was empty. Tony was due to be released tomorrow, she recalled, however, and there was probably a lot of last-minute preparations to make.

She sat down on the leather couch and began to leaf idly through a magazine just to use up the time. It was Sunday, and the base was deserted, utterly quiet outside except for the low, continual pounding of the surf. In a few moments, she began to feel restless. She set down the magazine and walked over to the window. When she glanced at her watch, she saw that only five minutes had passed. Where was everybody?

She began to pace around the small room. She thought about going home tomorrow, back to her house, her friends—her parents! What would she tell them? She could just hear her father's voice: 'You mean to say you saw him once, then just gave up? You didn't even bother to say goodbye to him?'

Suddenly it began to seem somewhat crass and unfeeling of her to leave like this without at least seeing him one more time. He didn't want her any more than she wanted him, but they had been married once, after all. They had been friends, even lovers. Perhaps she should at least say goodbye to him, wish him well.

I'll do it, she decided. She went out into the wide, empty corridor and started walking. It had seemed pretty straightforward the day Captain Jacobson had taken her to his room. She turned the corner at the end of the hall. Second room on the right, she recalled.

At the door, she hesitated, remembering how Tony had sent her away that first day. Nobody likes rejection, she thought. What if he does it again? Then she shrugged. Well, so what if he does? She still had to make this last token gesture of goodwill.

She raised her hand to knock, but before she did, her eye was caught by a glimpse of movement inside through the small window set in the door. She moved closer to get a better look, then dropped her hand and stared, transfixed by what she saw there.

Tony was sitting on the edge of the bed, his upper body bare, a sheet draped loosely around his hips. Kneeling on the bed behind him was a woman, a nurse or therapist of some kind, wearing a white uniform. She was leaning over him, her hands on his shoulders, kneading gently, her head close to his so that her long straight blonde hair fell in a curtain over her face.

Tony had his head bent, his eyes closed, as she massaged his shoulders and back, and Diana was struck dumb at the change in him. He was still very thin, she could see, but the pasty skin was now bronzed to a deep golden tan, the muscles of his arms and back looked firm and taut, and the black hair gleamed healthily in the shaft of sunlight coming in through the open window.

Diana caught her breath at the sight, hardly able to believe the transformation two weeks had wrought in him. And as she stared, a faint glimmer of remembrance began to stir within her, a growing sense of recognition, of familiarity with that face, that lithe body, even the way he sat, with his long hair-roughened legs dangling over the edge of the bed, his arms braced beside his hips.

Then he raised his head and turned it slightly in her direction, smiling up at the blonde, as though at a shared joke, and Diana's heart caught in her throat. It was *Tony* sitting there! The man was no longer a stranger, but Tony! *Her* Tony!

Her pulse began to pound as floods of long-repressed memory washed through her. Tony resplendent in his dress whites at their wedding, the broad grin on his handsome young face, the flashing white teeth. Tony on their wedding night, hovering over her on the bed, his broad shoulders bare, gazing down at her with the light of desire gleaming in his deep-brown eyes.

Then the telegram had come, the call from Captain Jacobson, and it was all over. He was dead. Her laughing, beautiful young husband would never return. After the first spasms of grief and loss, she had pushed all memory, all thought of him, out of her mind. She'd had to, merely to survive, and she'd managed to keep it there, buried, for seven long years.

As she continued to gaze inside the room, the blonde woman in there with him pushed back the curtain of hair so that Diana had a clear view of her face. She was smiling and gazing fondly down at the dark-haired man. She was very lovely.

Diana's cheeks burned. That's my husband she's pawing! she thought angrily. She took a deep breath to calm herself, then tapped lightly on the door and slowly pushed it open.

They both looked up as she entered the room. When he saw her, Tony's eyes narrowed, and the smile faded. The blonde gave her one guilty look, then backed hastily off the bed and got to her feet on the opposite side.

'Good morning, Mrs Hamilton,' she said, walking towards her. 'I'm Anne Scott, Tony's physical therapist.' She extended her hand, apparently recovering her poise, and gave Diana a cool appraising glance. 'We weren't expecting you.'

'No,' said Diana, taking the blonde's hand briefly, then dropping it. 'I can see that,' she added. Then she smiled. 'If you're through, would you mind leaving us alone for a while?' she asked pleasantly. 'I have some things I'd like to discuss in private with my husband,' she added, with a slight emphasis on the last word.

The blonde's gaze faltered at that, and she darted a quick glance at the man on the bed. He nodded shortly.

'I've had enough for now, Anne,' he said.

When they were alone, Diana wasn't quite sure how to start or even what she wanted to convey to the silent man who sat immovable on the edge of the bed. He hadn't changed his position. He just sat there, naked except for the loose sheet covering his mid-section, eyeing her thoughtfully.

'I thought you'd be gone by now,' he said at last. There was no hostility in his tone, but no genuine interest, either.

Diana walked over to the window and stood gazing out at the sloping lawn for several moments, searching for the right words. How could she tell him that she'd suddenly recognised him, that the past had once again become a living reality to her? What if he rejected her again? Two weeks ago, it hadn't really mattered. Now it did.

She turned around to face him. 'I thought we should talk first,' she said. Now it seemed as though the stranger was back, and she faltered, confused. 'We are still legally married, after all.'

He nodded. 'Yes. Well, you can do what you please about that.'

'I intend to,' she said sharply, and his dark eyes widened with a sudden flash of life. 'But first, I'd like to know what your wishes are in the matter.'

'I have no wishes in the matter,' he said promptly.

In spite of the innocuous statement, she had the odd sensation that he was deliberately challenging her, even testing her. It was then that she noticed the scars on his back, and she drew in her breath sharply at the sight of the angry welts, still visible under his newly-acquired tan.

'Not a pretty sight, are they?' he asked casually.

She tore her eyes away from them to meet his mocking gaze. As she watched, he slid his legs up on the bed and under the sheet, then sat up with his head resting on the pillows, effectively hiding his scarred back from her.

'I earned them, Diana. Every ugly mark.' His voice was low and bitter, and a spasm of pain passed over his hardened features. He turned his head away from her, as though unable to bear her horrified gaze. 'I don't want your pity,' he muttered. 'Why don't you go on home like a good little girl?'

'I'm sorry,' she said stiffly. 'It won't happen again.' She hesitated. 'Is that what you want, Tony?' she asked at last. 'For me to go home?'

His head moved around slowly to face her again. 'I

told you. Suit yourself. It doesn't matter to me one way or the other.'

Something told her he was lying, but she couldn't figure out why. Did he actually want her to stay, but was leaving her free to make her own decision? Or did he really want her to leave, but didn't like to say so?

Finally she decided to take him at his word. He really didn't care what she did. In that case, she'd . . . But what did she want? She stood there in confusion. When she'd watched him through the window, seen him smile at Anne Scott, he had seemed like the old Tony again. Her heart had gone out to him. Hope had flared up in her, a faint trace of the love she had once felt for him.

Now he was a stranger to her once again, his brown eyes cold and hard, his manner distant, and her determination to leave, to put an end to the past, was renewed. Still, she wasn't sure.

'All right,' she said at last, walking to the door, 'I'll do that. I'll just suit myself.'

It wasn't until the car arrived back at the hotel, less than half an hour later, that Diana actually made up her mind. Until then, she had sat silently next to the solemn-faced Mr Lindstrom, debating within herself, weighing the pros and cons either way.

Finally, she realised that there was no way to determine the proper course to take on a rational basis. She'd have to do exactly what she had told Tony she would do—suit herself. In other words, she thought grimly, operate on sheer instinct, plunge into the murky waters of the unknown, and hope she didn't drown.

When the car pulled up at the kerb, Mr Lindstrom turned to her. 'Well, Mrs Hamilton,' he said, not unkindly, but with no real warmth, 'you'll be leaving tomorrow, so I guess this is goodbye.' He held out a hand.

'No,' she said abruptly, ignoring the outstretched hand. She drew in a lungful of air. 'I've changed my mind.'

The agent's inscrutable grey eyes flew open, his jaw dropped, and Diana felt a surge of intense satisfaction to see this imperturbable man taken off guard at last.

Immediately, however, the eyes narrowed and the jaw snapped shut. He nodded once briefly, the old detached expression firmly back in place.

'You've changed your mind,' he repeated flatly.

She nodded. 'Yes. I've decided to go to Kauai after all.'

'Might I ask why the sudden about face?' he enquired drily.

'I can't really answer that. I just—back there at the hospital——' she faltered. 'Today, I felt that I was seeing Tony, my husband, for the first time since this whole thing began.' She shrugged helplessly. 'It's hard to explain. I'm sure you can't understand. Before, you were all pushing me into marriage with a stranger, and I was frightened.'

'Well, Mrs Hamilton, whether I understand or not is unimportant.' His voice was brisk, businesslike. 'What's essential is that you have changed your mind, and I've got some phone calls to make to get things organised. I assume you're all ready to go?'

She nodded. 'I was leaving on the first flight out early tomorrow morning. I've already packed.'

'All right. I'll leave you now. Cancel your reservation and check out of the hotel. I'll get back to you in an hour or two. There's no reason why we can't fly you to Kauai this afternoon. Everything there is ready anyway, since Tony is expected tomorrow. I'll arrange for a car at the Kauai airport,' he began ticking off on his fingers. 'I can get you Navy transport from Honolulu this afternoon. There's a gardener and a housekeeper already there, a Hawaiian couple who live in the native village nearby.'

He reached across her to open her door. She stepped out on to the pavement and had just started towards the entrance to the hotel when she heard him call her name. She turned around. He was leaning over the seat, his head at the open door.

'Mrs Hamilton,' he repeated, 'are you sure?'

'No,' she said. 'No, I'm not.' She smiled at the look of consternation in his face. 'But I guess I've got to give it a try, haven't I?'

Four hours later, she was driving up a narrow paved road towards the house on Kauai. It had been a short, uneventful flight from Honolulu, and the rental car had been waiting for her at the tiny airport.

The directions she had been given were quite simple to follow. It was a small circular island, set like a round emerald in the blue sea, with lush natural greenery abounding everywhere. The house itself was a low, rather sprawling structure, built of native wood and directly facing a private beach. Mr Lindstrom had told her that the nearest neighbours were two miles away on either side, so they would have all the privacy they needed.

Diana parked the car in front of the house and stepped out into the most beautiful garden she had ever seen. Surrounding the property was a thick growth of tropical trees, all strange to her, but which she later learned were candlenut, monkey pod and sandalwood. There were brilliant hibiscus, bougainvillaea and oleander blooming, and the heavy scent of the colourful blooms hung on the air.

It was late afternoon. The native couple had been notified of her arrival so that everything should be in order for her. She'd been told that they always left around two o'clock, but that there was plenty of food stocked in the kitchen for her supper.

It was cool and quiet inside the house. Most of the walls on the beach side were made of glass, but the blinds were all drawn, thin wooden slats that let in very little light. It was quite a large house, she saw as she walked around exploring, but contained very few rooms. A huge main room off the entrance foyer that looked out over the beach. A wide lanai attached, with a wooden railing around it and two steps leading down to a shimmering outdoor pool.

She went down a wide dim corridor. There were two very large bedrooms, both of them with sea views and both with their own adjacent bathrooms. One of the bedrooms was full of signs of male occupancy, she saw. There were men's shirts and trousers hanging in the cupboard and underwear folded neatly in the dresser drawers. Shaving gear was set out on the bathroom counter. Obviously, this had been prepared for Tony. He had come out of prison with nothing, and would need all new clothes and toilet articles.

Diana hesitated inside the room, her small overnight case in one hand, her bag slung over her shoulder, debating what to do. No, she decided finally. I'm not ready to share a bedroom with him, even if he is still my husband. She remembered, too, Tony's lack of warmth towards her, and knew that it would be a violation of his own privacy if she were simply to move into his bedroom first thing.

As she went back into the corridor, she realised that she didn't really know what to expect from this whole peculiar situation. She had made her decision to come here on an impulse, believing intuitively that it was worth a try.

She put her overnight case on the bed, opened it, and slowly started to unpack. Suddenly she felt very alone in the big empty house. What was she doing here, she thought in a rising panic, thousands of miles from home, in a strange place, waiting for an unknown man who was supposed to be her husband! She must have been out of her mind to come here! Tony himself obviously didn't want her. Not once had he shown the remotest sign of warmth towards her.

She sat down on the edge of the bed, her hands clutched in her lap. Had she done the right thing, she wondered, or made a terrible mistake? She didn't even know this man. He could be a dangerous lunatic for all she knew. After the long ordeal he'd been through, anything was possible.

Then she recalled the warm glow in his eyes, the wide smile, when he had looked up at Anne Scott that morning during the therapy session she had interrupted. I want him to look at *me* that way, she thought fiercely. Maybe it would be all right after all. The tension slowly began to leak away.

Look at the improvement in him in just two weeks, she rationalised as she went back out to the car to get her other luggage. He'll keep getting better, and eventually the suffering he had endured would become only a dim memory. They could go back home and resume their old life again just where they'd left off.

She would just have to be patient with him, she decided, as she lugged the heavier of the two suitcases into the house. And in time, with luck, her happy, light-hearted husband would be returned to her.

That night, after a light supper of fresh pineapple and a tasty fish salad she found in the refrigerator of the well-appointed kitchen, Diana decided to call her parents. She hadn't spoken to them for several days, and she should inform them of her plans.

Her mother answered the phone, and after Diana had told her where she was and that she'd be staying indefinitely, the inevitable question arose.

'And how is Tony?' her mother asked in a rather hushed, expectant voice.

'He's much better,' Diana replied truthfully. 'He's gained weight and got a tan. He's much stronger, too, with the physical therapy he's been getting.'

'That's wonderful. How does he seem otherwise? I mean, mentally?'

'It's hard to tell,' Diana said guardedly. 'I think those scars might take a little longer to heal, but there's a definite improvement there, too.'

'How about you? Are you all right, dear?'

Diana could sense the concern in her mother's voice. 'Oh, yes. I'm fine. The weather is gorgeous and we have a perfectly beautiful house, right on the beach. It's very quiet, very private, and we have a native couple to help us.'

'That's good,' came the relieved response. 'Well, keep

us informed, dear. We're both very proud of you. I know this can't have been easy for you. I'm glad you called.' Then, just as Diana was about to hang up, her mother said, 'Oh, I almost forgot. The Pattersons have rented a house on Kauai for the winter. I'm sure they'd love to see you and Tony.'

'It's a little too soon for that, Mother,' Diana said firmly. The Pattersons were old friends of the family, a retired Navy commander and his wife, with grown children. 'Maybe in a few weeks. It will depend on how Tony's convalescence progresses.'

They said goodbye then and hung up.

Diana felt much better for having talked to her mother, not quite so alone. It will be all right, she told herself as she got ready for bed that night. It has to be.

When Captain Jacobson and Tony arrived the next afternoon, Diana was standing out on the wide covered front porch waiting for them. She had spent the morning in nervous anticipation, and sent Tomo and Leia, the native couple, home early. She'd tried on several different dresses. One seemed too severe, another too casual, another too sexy, until finally she just left on a simple cotton sundress of a bright coral colour and a pair of flat-heeled sandals as the best she could do.

What would Tony say when he saw her there? she wondered as she watched the car driving up the road towards the house. But then surely he knew. Captain Jacobson or Mr Lindstrom would have told him. But maybe not. Maybe he just would have taken it for granted that she'd gone back to Seattle and the subject hadn't even come up.

When the car came to a halt, she put on a broad smile

of welcome and started walking slowly towards it. The older man got out first, then walked around the front of the car to help Tony, but before he got there, Tony had opened the door himself and stepped out on to the pavement.

When he looked at her, she knew instantly that he was surprised to see her. His eyes widened momentarily, and for one second she was certain she saw a gleam of pleasure in the brown depths, but then it was gone and the familiar closed-in look was back.

'Diana,' he said, walking slowly towards her. 'I see you're all settled in.'

There was no way to see whether he was glad to see her or not. The inscrutable mask gave away nothing. He looked wonderful, she thought with a little catch in her throat, tall and bronzed by the sun, the dark hair neatly cut and gleaming with life.

He was wearing well fitting tan cotton shorts and a white knitted shirt, and although he was still thin, his face still gaunt, the firmed-up muscle structure of his chest and shoulders was clearly visible under the thin shirt.

'I'll get your bags, Tony,' the Captain called to him. He opened the back door of the car and reached inside.

A look of irritation crossed Tony's face. 'I can do that, Arne,' he said.

They argued for a moment, then compromised by each carrying a bag. Diana led them into the house and down the corridor to Tony's room. By the time he set his bag down on the bed, a sheen of perspiration had broken out on his forehead and his hands were trembling.

He's still so weak, Diana thought as she watched him trying to cover his obvious exhaustion. Leaving the hospital, the plane ride, the drive from the airport, all had taken their toll.

Arne Jacobson had obviously noticed it, too. After one sharp glance, he'd fished in his pocket and come out with a small white packet.

'I have strict orders, Tony,' he said in a severe tone, 'to see to it that you take this pill the moment we arrive and lie down.'

Tony frowned, and Diana could see the struggle going on inside him. Then he smiled crookedly and reached for the packet.

'Aye, aye, sir,' he murmured, and ripped it open.

'I'll get a glass of water,' said Diana, making towards the bathroom.

He frowned again. 'I can do that,' he said curtly.

'Well,' came the Captain's hearty voice, 'I expect we'd better leave him alone, Diana.' He held out a hand. 'I'll say goodbye, then, Tony. Call me if you need anything. And let me know when you decide on your answer.'

Tony took his hand and shook it. 'I will, Arne, and thanks for everything.'

Diana and the Captain left him, then, and as they walked towards the large main room, Diana turned to him.

'Won't you stay for supper, Captain?' she asked politely. 'Or a drink at least?'

He shook his head firmly. 'No. I've been away from Washington for two weeks now, and have to get back.' He gave her a brief, warm smile. 'Besides, it's best for you two to be alone for a while.'

She walked out to the car with him, half glad he was leaving, yet half sorry, too. She did want to be alone with Tony, but she was a little bit afraid of him at the same time. There had been no warmth in his greeting. Was he sorry she had decided to come, or merely indifferent?

Before he got inside the car, he turned to her. 'Tony and I had a long talk on our way over here,' he said gravely. 'I want him back on active duty as soon as possible. I've talked it over with my superiors, and also with your father, and they concur with my opinion. I'd like your help.'

She gave him a worried look. 'But it's too soon! You saw how weak he is.'

He nodded. 'Yes, but he's light years ahead of where he was two weeks ago. He's basically strong, just needs a little more fattening up, exercise, rest. There's nothing physically wrong with him.' He reddened slightly and lowered his eyes to the ground. 'The doctors say he's totally viable in every respect, that there's no activity he can't indulge in, in moderation.' He gave her an enquiring glance. 'If you understand what I mean.'

Sex, she thought. He's talking about sex. 'Yes,' she said, 'I understand.'

'Good.' He slid behind the wheel and gazed up at her through the open car window. 'Can I count on you, Diana? Will you help to persuade him to go back on active status in the Navy as soon as he's well enough?'

'Yes, of course.' Diana thought of the life they'd led before Tony was 'killed', the military life she had known since she was born, and which she had continued to live even as a widow. She was used to it. She enjoyed it, the travel, the parties, the sense of belonging to a small élite group, the friends encountered over and over again all over the world. And with Tony back to share it with her, it would be even better. 'It's what I want anyway,' she added.

With a smile of satisfaction and a little salute, he started the engine and backed the car around. She stood in the driveway and watched him until he was out of sight. Then she turned and walked into the house.

CHAPTER FOUR

BY seven o'clock that evening, Diana was beginning to grow seriously worried. There hadn't been a sound from Tony's bedroom since Captain Jacobson had left. Every half-hour or so, she would tiptoe down the corridor and stand listening at his door, but the only sound to be heard was the relentless pounding of the surf in the background.

What if he'd had a relapse? she wondered as she made yet another trip down the hall to his room. What if he was lying unconscious in there and needed help? They had said he was all right, but that was when he was safely in the hospital, under constant observation. Now she had sole responsibility for him. What should she do?

Leia had left another cold supper, and Diana was starved. She'd either have to wake him or eat alone. Finally, she decided she would have to risk his annoyance. It would have to be better than this helpless anxiety. She raised her hand and tapped lightly on the door.

'Tony,' she called. 'Would you like some supper?'

There was a long silence, and she was just about to knock again when she heard him speak.

'Yes, please,' came the reply. 'Give me fifteen minutes to clean up, okay?'

'Yes, of course.'

She was so relieved at the calm, matter-of-fact tone in his voice that she started to hum lightly under her breath as she walked back to the kitchen. Regardless of how he felt about her presence in the house, apparently he wasn't going to cause any difficulty over it or make her uncomfortable.

They would get reacquainted, she thought, as she set the table out on the lanai. They had both changed in seven years, naturally, but were still basically the same people. They had cared enough about each other to fall in love and marry, she reasoned, and they owed it to themselves at least to give it a try.

Besides, she had to admit she was attracted to Tony, not so much because he had been her husband in the past, but because of what he had become. The boy he had been before and the man he was now could be two different people. She had adored the young Tony Hamilton, but he had largely been a flattering reflection of herself. This new Tony was stronger, somehow, in spite of his physical weakness, even forbidding, and she dimly sensed that his love would have to be earned.

Everything was on the table now, and she stood at the railing of the lanai gazing out at the blue sea. The sun was to her left and sinking fast, casting a wide golden swathe over the darkening water. Down on the shore she could see several large birds waddling up and down, scavenging for shellfish on the beach and making a peculiar honking sound.

'That's the *nene* bird,' came a quiet voice behind her. 'A form of goose. Hawaii's state bird.'

She turned around. Tony was standing a foot or so away from her. He looked rested, she thought. The hollows in his cheeks had begun to fill out, and the dark circles under his eyes were gone. He was wearing another knitted shirt, a pale yellow, and she could smell the clean scent of soap from his shower. His dark hair was still a little damp.

'That's interesting,' she said inanely, just to be saying something.

She knew she was staring at him, but she couldn't help herself. It was the first time they had really been alone together since that first awful meeting at the hospital, and she was a little nervous.

'I had a lot of time on my hands the past few weeks,' he explained with an offhand shrug of his wide shoulders, 'so I boned up on Hawaiian flora and fauna.'

She'd forgotten how tall he was. When he was so ill, he had been in bed and was so thin that he seemed almost frail. Now, with his strength returning, his presence was more formidable.

'Shall we sit down?' she asked brightly, moving away from him. 'Are you hungry? I got out some chilled wine, but then I wondered if you were well enough . . .'

'I'm perfectly well,' came the sharp reply. 'I can eat and drink whatever I like. The wine sounds like a good idea.'

They sat down then, and while Diana dished up the food, Tony uncorked the wine and poured it out. They started eating without another word spoken between them. Diana was hurt by his abrupt tone, his sudden withdrawal, his morose silence. Why was he so touchy? If he didn't want her there, why didn't he just say so? She'd never forced herself on a man yet, and she wasn't going to start now.

Her thoughts began building gradually towards a state of righteous indignation, and she was just about to open her mouth to tell him what was on her mind, when he spoke at last.

'I was surprised to see you here, Diana,' he said quietly. 'What made you decide to come?'

She laid her fork down carefully on her plate and took a sip of wine to calm herself before replying. Then she gave him a cool, direct look.

'I'm not sure now,' she said in a tight voice. 'If you didn't want me to come, you should have said so yesterday when we discussed it.'

'I didn't say I didn't want you here.' His voice was low and controlled. 'I told you I wanted you to suit yourself.'

'Then why the surprise?' she snapped.

He leaned back in his chair in a relaxed posture and gazed steadily at her for a long moment. Then he said, 'Let's be honest, Diana. I wasn't so sick that first day you came to the hospital that I didn't see quite clearly you were there under protest.'

She reddened and tried to think of a suitable reply, but he was right, after all. She remained silent.

'I can just hear your father,' he went on. 'It's your duty, Diana,' he mimicked in a ponderous tone. 'It was written all over your face. You didn't want a broken-down husband returned from the grave, any more than I wanted . . .' He broke off then.

'Any more than you wanted a wife?' she finished softly.

'All right,' he said. 'Any more than I wanted a wife.' He leaned forward now, his elbows on the table, and fixed her with a penetrating stare. 'It's been seven years!' he ground out. 'Seven long years! We were children. You've had your own life during all that time, and I've had mine, such as it was. It's insane to think we can just turn the clock back.'

'I take it then, that you don't even want to try,' she said.

Tony spread his hands in a helpless gesture. 'What's the point? You don't even know me. The years I spent in prison . . . ' The haunted look was back in his eyes. 'Well, they changed me in a fundamental way.'

'I see.' Diana sat quite still while she pondered his remarks, but her hands twisted nervously in her lap, out of sight. She had just about decided to tell him she'd leave the next day, when a sudden thought occured to her.

'You're in love with Anne Scott, aren't you?' she asked quietly, and was astonished at the sick sensation in the pit of her stomach this realisation gave her.

He stared blankly at her for a moment, then threw back his head and laughed, a harsh, hollow laugh, with no merriment in it. When he spoke again, his voice was gentler, and there was a softer light in the deep brown eyes.

'Believe me, Diana,' he said with conviction, love is the last thing on my mind. I'm only interested in one thing—survival.'

He poured himself another glass of wine, then got up from his chair and went to the railing. He stood there gazing out at the sea, a deep blue now that the sun had set. It was growing chilly, and Diana shivered a little in her thin cotton dress.

She felt oddly let down, almost depressed, a state of mind so foreign to her sunny nature that it frightened her a little. Except for her sudden widowhood, so long ago, she had lived a charmed life, with everything she'd ever wanted coming easily and naturally to her. She had automatically assumed that if she wanted Tony, he would want her, and she simply wasn't equipped to deal with his patent indifference.

He turned then, and gazed down at her. It had grown quite dark by now, with only a pale crescent moon to light the sky. She couldn't make out the expression on his face, but when he spoke, the voice was kind.

'What about you, Diana?' he asked. 'Surely you haven't spent the last seven years grieving for me, in a state of perpetual mourning? You're very beautiful, even more so than I remembered. Why haven't you married again?'

'I don't know,' she said honestly. 'I just never felt the urge. I liked my life the way it was.'

'Surely you had opportunities,' he persisted. 'Dan Armstrong, for example. He was in love with you even before we were married.'

'I like Dan,' she said slowly. 'He's been very kind, very attentive. I guess I even love him in a way,' she added. 'But not enough to marry him.'

'But he's asked you,' came the insistent voice.

'Yes. He's asked,' she admitted.

There was a long silence then, and finally Diana got up and started to clear the table. She turned on the light in the kitchen and carried the left-over food and dishes inside. As she rinsed them at the sink and stacked them in the dishwasher, she wondered what she should do.

Nothing had been resolved. Perhaps it would be best if she just left tomorrow, went back to Seattle, picked up her life where she left off, and forgot any of this happened. Tony didn't want her in his life, that much was clear. He'd said it himself. What was the point?

Yet there was another aspect to consider. Should he be left alone? He had been released from hospital in her care. What if she did go and something happened to him? He seemed strong enough now and able to care for himself with the help of Leia and Tomo. If she left the island, would the Navy send someone to look after him? Anne Scott, perhaps?

She dried her hands carefully and hung the towel on the rack underneath the sink. She didn't care for that idea at all. Anne Scott and Tony alone in the house. Just then, he came inside, closing the glass door behind him. Diana turned to face him.

'Do you want me to leave, Tony?' she asked point blank.

'I think it would be the wise thing to do,' he replied at once. 'For your sake.' Then he smiled crookedly and ran a hand through his dark hair. 'It's a funny thing about marriage, though,' he mused thoughtfully. 'Something oddly permanent and irrevocable about it. I didn't take it lightly then, and I still don't.'

'Neither do I,' she said, her spirits suddenly soaring, as though a great weight had been lifted from her heart.

'Well then, no, I don't want you to leave. If you like, we can just take it one day at a time, see what happens.'

He left the kitchen, and she could hear him walking down the corridor to his bedroom. He didn't want her to leave, she thought, and that was something. Then she frowned. Passively not wanting her to leave and actively wanting her to stay were two entirely different things. And even though his fine words about the permanency of marriage had warmed her heart, she knew they were only abstract, theoretical, and she hadn't missed the very real tone of hopelessness in his voice even as he spoke them.

From that night on, they didn't speak of their

relationship again. Their days fell naturally into a pattern. Tony rose early to jog along the beach, going a little further each day. Then after an hour or so in the surf, he would swim several laps in the pool by the lanai, both for exercise and to wash off the salt water.

Diana was a late riser, and by the time she had showered and dressed, Tony would already have had his breakfast, an enormous meal, prepared happily by the adoring Leia. He would disappear into his room then, just as Diana appeared in the kitchen for her own breakfast, and she wouldn't see him again until late afternoon.

She presumed he was still resting a lot, shut up in his bedroom like that for hours at a time, but occasionally she would hear him pacing back and forth when she walked by, and later on, the clack of a typewriter. He never told her what he was doing.

In the late afternoon, he would emerge for another walk and swim. He never asked her to go with him, and she didn't like to invite herself. They would meet for a late supper, where their conversation was desultory and superficial, interspersed with long awkward silences.

Several times during that week, she had tried to question him about his experiences in prison, but a hard mask would settle on his face, and he would change the subject. Finally, he told her curtly that he had strict orders from the Navy not to discuss that, not even with her, and she dropped the subject.

After a week of this, Diana was bored out of her mind. She'd read every magazine in the house from cover to cover and even driven into the nearby town for more. She swam and walked on the beach herself while Tony was shut away in his room, and tried to help Leia with the cooking and cleaning or Tomo with the garden, but they both just grinned at her, shook their heads vehemently, and politely shooed her away.

What she longed for, she realised, was some human companionship. Not only was she sick to death of her own company, she was also beginning to grow angry. From the beginning, her theory in dealing with Tony had been to leave him alone, to make no demands on him, to allow him to come to her of his own accord.

But this was getting ridiculous, she grumbled to herself one night as she set the table for their supper out on the lanai. For all the communication they had, she might as well be there alone. It was time she stopped walking on eggs around him and started to think about what *she* wanted.

Well, she thought, pausing in the midst of setting out the silverware, what do I want? I want a husband, came the immediate silent answer. I want companionship, affection, caring. I want love.

Day by day, as Tony grew stronger, she found herself more and more attracted to him. His bronzed body glowed with health now, and there was a spring to his step, a new sparkle in his eyes. Occasionally, watching him out of her bedroom window in the morning as he swam his laps in the pool, she longed to go to him, to join him there, to feel those long muscular arms around her, the sensuous mouth on hers.

Is that what's making me so restless? she wondered. She stood stock still, the silverware still in her hands, thinking it over carefully. Then she made up her mind. She'd just have to seduce him.

In the days that followed, she tried everything. She got

up an hour earlier and met Tony at the pool when he came out of the surf, wearing the scantiest bikini she owned. She managed to brush against him while she was clearing the table after dinner. She discarded her bras, and wore all her lowest-cut dresses.

All her efforts evoked in him was a quizzical look and a polite, rather bemused acceptance. Is he made of stone? she fumed to herself late one afternoon a few days after she'd started her abortive campaign. Had something happened in prison, some injury that made him impotent?

No, she thought. He would have told her. She recalled her last conversation with Captain Jacobson, his evident embarrassment when he'd assured her Tony was perfectly normal and capable of *any* activity. The meaning had been clear.

She was out on the lanai, lounging on one of the chaise-longues and leafing idly through another boring magazine. Tony was in the pool having his afternoon swim. She threw the magazine aside and walked over to the railing to watch him. He had just finished his last lap and was sitting on the edge of the pool, flexing his shoulders back and forth, as though to loosen them. Diana stood there and stared at the taut muscles rippling under the smooth skin, the scars barely visible now under the heavy tan, and a slow warmth began to steal through her.

Suddenly he turned around. Their eyes met and held in a long look, and she was certain at that moment that he desired her. He rose to his feet and started walking slowly towards her, his steady gaze never faltering. Her heart began to pound, a wave of dizziness passed over her, and she clung to the wooden railing for support.

He's coming to me at last! she thought joyfully.

Just then the front doorbell rang. Leia and Tomo had already left, so she would have to answer it herself. For a moment she was tempted to ignore it, but at the sound Tony had dropped his eyes and quickened his step.

He was beside her now, looking down at her. 'Better see who it is, I guess,' he said.

'Yes.' Diana turned her head to hide her disappointment. 'I guess I'd better.'

He followed her into the house and stood back in the large main room watching her as she went into the foyer to answer the door. Still annoyed at the untimely interruption, she yanked it open to see a grinning Dan Armstrong standing on the doorstep.

'Dan!' she exclaimed, and fell into his arms with a glad cry. 'It's so wonderful to see you! What are you doing here?'

She hadn't realised until that moment how much she missed the sight of a friendly face. She kissed him affectionately on the cheek, then, with one arm still around his waist, turned to Tony. He was walking slowly towards them, the brown eyes taking in the scene.

He held out a hand. 'It's good to see you again, Dan.'

Dan stared at him for a moment, then dropped his arm from Diana's shoulders. He took Tony's hand in both of his and pumped it enthusiastically.

'My God, old buddy!' he said fervently. 'If you aren't a sight for sore eyes!'

'Dan, will you please tell me what in the world you're doing on Kauai?' asked Diana, leading the way into the living-room.

'I'm staying with the Pattersons, just on the other side of the island. A little vacation.' He glanced at Tony.

'Although I was hoping to get a glimpse of our conquering hero, I'll have to admit.'

'You don't really believe all that garbage you read in the newspapers, do you, Dan?' Tony asked lightly.

Dan chuckled. 'Of course not.' He gave Tony a light punch on the arm. 'I know you too well.'

Tony grinned. 'How about a drink?'

'Oh, yes,' Diana agreed. 'Let's all have one. Can you stay for dinner?'

'I'll have one quick drink,' said Dan, 'but I won't stay.' He gave Tony a fond look. 'Actually, I just wanted to see for myself that it really was you, that you really were still alive.' He shook his head. 'I still can't believe it.'

'Sit down, Dan,' invited Diana. 'I'm dying to hear all the news from home.' She walked over to the drinks cupboard in the corner of the large room. 'Do you want your usual gin and tonic?' she asked, reaching for glasses. 'Tony,' she called over her shoulder, 'what would you like?'

There was a short silence, then he said, 'Sure. Gin and tonic sounds fine. I'll go and get some ice.'

'Oh, I'll do that.'

'I can manage a tray of ice, Diana,' Tony said in a tight voice. He turned to Dan. 'She insists on treating me like an invalid.'

'Well you've got to admit, Tony,' said Dan, sitting down on the edge of the couch, 'you've been through a pretty gruelling ordeal.'

Tony made a brief gesture of dismissal. 'I'm okay now, though.'

He went into the kitchen for the ice. While he was gone, Diana carried their drinks over to the coffee-table in front of the couch and sat down next to Dan.

'How is he really?' he asked in a low voice.

'I'm not sure,' she said slowly. 'Physically, he's fine. But he's still very withdrawn. I don't know. How does he seem to you?'

Dan thought a minute. 'Older, of course, and, as you say, somewhat withdrawn, remote. But he looks good.' He gave her a sharp, enquiring look. 'How about you? This whole thing can't have been easy for you.'

Before she could answer, Tony was back with the ice. He put some in each glass, then emptied the tray into the metal ice-bucket and sat down in a chair across from the couch.

'Now, tell me what's been going on in Seattle,' said Diana, settling back on the couch with her legs tucked underneath her. 'I want to know everything. Did you go to the Madisons' party on New Year's Day? It's the first one I've missed in years.' She laughed. 'I don't even know who won the Rose Bowl.'

They chatted for half an hour, Dan filling Diana in on their mutual friends and Tony remaining largely silent, watching them. Diana glanced his way occasionally, trying to include him in the conversation, giving him a little background on the people. He seemed perfectly relaxed and content to sit quietly, sipping his drink and smiling politely, while she and Dan chattered.

Finally Dan drained the last of his drink and rose to his feet. 'I'd better be on my way. Don't want to outstay my welcome on my first visit.'

'Nonsense,' Tony said warmly, as though he really meant it. 'It's great to see you again. We'll have to get together soon for a real visit.'

'Well, the Pattersons have a houseful of people staying with them.' Dan mentioned several names familiar to

Diana. 'And there's a continual party going on. They're all anxious to see you, Tony.'

'We'll have to arrange something soon,' Tony murmured.

'Oh, yes,' Diana agreed warmly. 'I'll call Janet Patterson soon and we'll set a date.'

As they walked into the foyer together, Dan turned to Tony. 'What are your plans? Arne Jacobson told me he was trying to talk you into going right back on active duty. Have you decided yet?'

'No, I haven't. Right now it doesn't appeal to me, but I'm trying to keep an open mind.'

'Can't ask fairer than that,' said Dan. He turned to Diana. 'Thanks for the drink. I'll probably be seeing you soon.' He leaned down to kiss her lightly on the cheek.

At the door, the two men shook hands warmly, then Tony and Diana stood watching as Dan walked out to his car. He turned to smile and wave at them, then got inside and drove off.

Diana felt a little let down when he was gone. It had been so good to see him again, she thought, as she closed the front door. Tony had gone on ahead back to the living-room. She wondered how he felt about Dan's visit. Although he had been very quiet, he did seem to be genuinely glad to see his old friend again.

She thought about the Pattersons, the people she knew who were staying with them, and her spirits rose. That was what they needed, she decided firmly, to get back into a normal social life again. She hadn't realised how much she'd missed it.

'It was good to see Dan again, wasn't it?' she asked when she came back into the living-room.

Tony was standing at the glass door to the lanai, his

back towards her, looking out. He turned around at her question and smiled at her. 'Yes,' he agreed, 'it was.'

She collected the glasses and put them on the tray. 'Do you find him changed?'

He thought a moment. 'Not really. Dan's a pretty solid type. He'll always be basically the same.'

'It'll be fun to get together with the Pattersons, too,' she went on cautiously.

'You miss that, don't you, Diana?'

She was halfway to the door of the kitchen and turned at the serious note in his voice. She searched his face, but all she saw there was a polite expectancy.

'Yes,' she said. 'Yes, I do.'

Tony nodded soberly and turned back to the sea, his hands shoved in his trousers pockets. Diana stood there, the tray in her hands, longing to go to him, to tell him that he was what she really cared about, far more than her friends, but he had shut her out again.

'He's still in love with you, you know,' he said in a low voice.

She opened her mouth to protest, to tell him that even if it were true, she didn't care, but the words wouldn't come.

He turned back to face her. 'He'd make a fine husband for you, Diana,' he said quietly.

'If I'd wanted Dan for a husband, I would have married him long ago, when I thought I was free,' she said in an even tone. 'Why should I want him now, when I already have a husband?'

She was about to add that he himself was the one she wanted if he would just give her a chance, but the grave expression on his face stopped her. Something was troubling him. If only he'd tell her! What did he want?

Was she just wasting her time trying to be a wife to him?

She turned, then, and continued on into the kitchen. He obviously wasn't going to reply to her question.

Lying in bed that night, dozing fitfully, Diana tried to sort out her conflicting emotions. Her mind kept returning to the moment she and Tony had shared that afternoon before Dan had rung the doorbell and destroyed the fragile tension between them. Then, later, after Dan left, he had retreated from her again.

Still, there was no mistaking the look in his eyes. It was the gleam of desire that had shone from them, she was convinced. Desire for her. More than anything, she wanted to resume her marriage, a real marriage, with her husband. All the old love and attraction she'd felt for him once had returned. If only he would bend a little, she reasoned, and trust her, they could have a wonderful life together. The seven years apart would be forgotten, and they could just take up where they'd left off.

She began to elaborate on the fantasy. They'd get back in the social swing first. The Pattersons' presence on the island was a heaven-sent opportunity for that. Then Tony would go on active duty again, maybe in Seattle. It didn't really matter. Wherever they were stationed, there would be people they knew, interesting places to see, new things to try.

Perhaps, some day, she mused dreamily, they might even consider having children. Not for a long time, but maybe eventually. She'd never wanted children before. There was always too much she'd wanted to do. Children tied you down. But with Tony, it might be a good way to consolidate the marriage.

Then she almost laughed aloud at the foolish castle in

the air she'd just built. Here she was planning a future that included children, when so far he couldn't even bring himself to touch her! Am I repulsive to him, in some way? she wondered. Sometimes he acted as though he resented her very presence in the house, even hated her.

Maybe she should just give up, leave the island, go back to Seattle, get her divorce. If only she had someone to confide in, she thought, someone to advise her. But there was no one. She would just have to work it out herself.

After another half-hour of tossing and turning and fruitless speculation, she switched on the lamp by the bed and got up. Maybe if she ate something she'd be able to sleep. The hell with her mother and her precious rule about not eating between meals, she thought recklessly. A fat lot of good her figure did her when it didn't even rouse a spark in her own husband!

Grumbling to herself, she padded barefoot down the hall towards the kitchen. Perhaps a breath of fresh air would help, she decided, and crossed through the main room to the sliding glass door that led to the lanai. Even before she reached it, however, she could see the tall figure of a man standing there.

She was startled at first, until she realised it was only Tony. Obviously, he couldn't sleep, either. She stood quite still for a moment, watching him through the open door. Her heart began to pound as an idea, just a bare suggestion, began to form in her mind. Something had to be done. She didn't know what, but something. Anything!

Tony was standing with his back towards her, his hands braced on the top of the wooden railing. His head was bent, and he seemed to be staring out at the phosphorescent waves breaking on the shore, deeply immersed in his own private, troubled thoughts. Her heart went out to him in a sudden surge of warmth and protectiveness. He needs me as much as I need him, she thought, and made up her mind.

Soundlessly, she started walking towards him.

CHAPTER FIVE

IN the dim glow cast by the pale half-moon, Diana could see the sharp line where the deep tan ended just below his waist, leaving a patch of blurry white on his slim hips before resuming at the top of his thighs.

At first she thought he was naked, and she paused, uncertain whether to go on, then she realised that he was wearing a pair of white jockey shorts, and she kept on, quietly, until she had passed through the open door and stepped silently out on to the lanai. She stood behind him, just two steps away, hesitating. If he had heard her, he gave no sign. He just continued to stand there motionless.

She had no idea what she was going to do next, but as her gaze travelled hungrily over the near-naked body, taking in the smooth muscled back, the narrow hips and long hair-roughened legs, a sudden heated spurt of desire took possession of her and gave her courage.

She took the two steps that separated them and pressed herself lightly up against him, barely touching him. She felt his body go rigid, saw his dark head come up, but he didn't pull away from her. She pressed a little closer, so that her breasts flattened on his bare back and she became almost painfully aware of how the hardening peaks thrust against his skin.

Still, Tony didn't move a muscle, except that his breathing had become more laboured. She slid her arms around him and laid one hand over his heart, which she could feel thudding wildly now under her touch. She laid her lips on his scarred back and began to move her fingers lightly over his chest, his ribcage, down over his flat stomach until she reached the waistband of his shorts.

The sensitive skin quivered under her feathery touch, and she hesitated. But before she could decide whether to explore his body further, he suddenly twisted around and grasped her by the shoulders. He stared down at her, the dark eyes boring into hers with a fierce, almost fanatical intensity. A spasm of pain crossed his face, and he ground out her name harshly. 'Diana!'

For a moment she was frightened by the wildly hungry look he gave her, but then her fear evaporated, and she held his gaze unflinching. Tony suddenly reached out and ripped her nightgown down the middle, pulling at the thin material until it lay in shreds on the deck.

Then his open mouth came down hard over hers, engulfing it in a hot moistness, his tongue pushing past her lips and teeth. His hands moved down feverishly over her breasts, her waist, paused between her legs, then clutched at her hips and pulled her up against his hard arousal.

Diana's blood sang in exultation. His punishing kiss ground her teeth into the inside of her mouth so that she could taste the blood, and he was crushing her so tightly against him that she felt the pain of it along the whole length of her body, but she didn't care.

She threw her arms around his neck and grasped the thick hair growing there. This was what she had been longing for, waiting for. Her whole being was alive, on fire, and she moved against him sensuously, invitingly.

Finally, his mouth never leaving hers, Tony put a knee on the chaise-longue behind her and eased her backwards until she was lying down and she could feel his weight settle on top of her. His breath was coming in great gasps now, and with a strangled sob he tore his lips from hers and raised himself up slightly to look down at her.

He lowered his head to her breast, then, and when she felt his lips pulling at the throbbing nipple, she sighed deeply and ran her hands up and down his back, underneath the shorts now, pushing them down further on his hips.

She heard him groan, deep in his throat, and he raised his head to claim her lips in another grinding, punishing kiss. At the same time, she arched herself up against him and felt him thrust into her. Then all thinking stopped as their body rhythms came together and rose to a pounding climax unlike anything she had ever experienced before in her life.

When it was over, Tony lay slumped against her, his breath still coming in short gasps. In a moment, he rolled over and lay on his back, one arm raised to cover his eyes. Diana's instinct told her to leave him alone for now, but when his breathing returned to normal, she lifted herself up on one elbow and leaned over him. Still not uttering a word, she reached out her free hand and began to stroke the dark hair back from his damp forehead.

At last he lowered his arm and gazed up at her. 'God, I'm sorry, Diana,' he said.

She smiled down at him. 'What for?' she asked, still stroking.

'For attacking you like some damned animal,' he

growled in disgust. 'I've dreamed about this for days, gone over and over it in my mind. I was going to be so gentle with you, take it so slow and easy.' He shook his head. 'It's just that it's been so long . . .' His voice trailed off.

Diana leaned down and kissed him on the mouth. 'But, darling, it's exactly what I wanted you to do. Why do you think I crept out here in the middle of the night if not to seduce you?'

He narrowed his eyes in disbelief. 'To seduce me? Are you serious?'

'Of course—I've been trying to do it subtly for days, and tonight, when I saw you out here, I decided that the direct approach was all that might work.'

'Well, I'll be damned,' Tony said admiringly. 'You little devil!'

She nodded happily. 'That's right.'

His gaze softened then. 'I thought about you so often when I was in prison.' He raised his hand and trailed his fingers through her hair, then over her face, lingering on every feature. 'I had your lovely face engraved on my memory.' His hand moved over her throat and settled on her breast. 'Your beautiful body,' he murmured, and began kneading gently.

Desire began to rise up in her again, warming her blood and drying her throat. Her eyes filled with tears.

'I love you, Tony,' she whispered. 'I love you.'

He sat up, then, and took her tenderly in his arms, his lips nuzzling her hair, her mouth, her cheek.

'God, Diana, I thought I'd never see you again. I was sure I'd lost you.' He began to murmur in her ear. 'Let's go to bed, Mrs Hamilton. This time I'll do it right.'

The next morning, Diana awoke beside her sleeping husband for the first time in seven years, just as the sun's first light began to filter through the thin wooden slats of the blinds at her bedroom window.

She was startled at first by the alien presence in her bed, but as she slowly came to full consciousness and recognised him, memory came flooding back. She smiled happily. True to his word, their second excursion into the joys of love had been quite different from that first explosive encounter.

She felt just like a warm contented cat, and she started to stretch lazily when it dawned on her that she might wake him if she moved. Here was an opportunity to watch him unobserved. Cautiously, she raised herself up on one elbow and leaned over him.

He was on his back, his head turned away from her on the pillow, one arm flung over his head, the other lying at his side. The thin sheet they'd slept under was down around his waist so that she had a clear view of his entire upper body.

He looks so vulnerable in repose, she thought. She stared, enchanted, at the steady rise and fall of his smooth tanned chest as he slept. The bony structure of his shoulders, arms and ribcage was still prominent, the stomach almost hollow, but there was also a fine padding of firm taut muscle covering it. He looked thin, but strong and supple from his disciplined exercise.

As she gazed at the straight nose, the firm chin and sensuous mouth of his profile, she wondered how she could ever have thought him a stranger. It was her own Tony lying there, and all the forgotten love she had once felt for him was back, filling her whole being with an intense, happy glow.

Yet, she thought, it really wasn't the Tony she remembered, not entirely. The new Tony had all the wonderful traits of the old one, but with something added, a maturity in the firm set of the mouth, a hint of suffering overcome around the eyes. If anything, she thought, with a fierce rush of love, he was better. The boy had become a man, and he belonged to her!

He still desired her, still loved her, too. She was certain of that. Even though he hadn't said it in words, he'd told her in every other way. She closed her eyes, suddenly weak with a spasm of powerful longing for him as she recalled the way his hands and mouth had worshipped her body last night.

She gazed at him again. Then, unable to stop herself, carried along by an irresistible momentum, she reached out to run two fingers over his body, trailing them lightly down from the long column of his throat until they slipped underneath the sheet and continued downwards to his thighs.

She was so absorbed in her fascinating exploration that she didn't realise he was awake and watching her until she felt his body shake with silent laughter.

'Mm,' he said with sleepy satisfaction. 'Waking up in prison was never like this!'

Immediately, she turned scarlet and started to snatch her hand away, but before she could move, his own hand clamped down on hers, forcing it to stay where it was.

'Don't,' he murmured. 'Leave it there.'

Their eyes met briefly, but then, as she saw his gaze shift lower, she turned an even deeper shade of red when she suddenly realised that she was naked. Her nightgown must still be lying in shreds on the lanai.

'Look at me,' he said. She obeyed. 'Don't ever be

embarrassed with me. You've got to trust me. Do you trust me, Diana?'

She didn't think she would be able to utter a coherent word, her throat was so tight and dry, so she only nodded. Tony smiled, then, and reached out a hand to run it back and forth over her firm bare breasts, the peaks coming alive under his sensitive fingers. Her hand tightened on him involuntarily, and she closed her eyes, drowning in pure sensation.

Both his hands were busy now, one still flicking lightly over her taut nipples, circling, playing, teasing, first one, then the other, while his other hand moved further down her body in a warm sensuous exploration of his own.

With a choking sound deep in his throat, he rolled her over on to her back. She threw her arms around his neck, and looked up at him. He was hovering over her, his chest heaving, the brown eyes deep and flaming with desire.

He kissed her then, his mouth opened wide, hot, moist, insistent, and pressing his body on top of hers, joined her again in another glorious journey to the supreme expression of love between a man and a woman.

She slept afterwards, a deep dreamless sleep of total content. When she awakened again, Tony was gone, and she could hear the low murmur of voices in another part of the house, then a door shutting, and the sound of a car driving away.

She stretched widely, pulled the sheet up over her shoulders, and lay back with her eyes closed again. Was it company at this hour of the morning? She didn't even know what time it was. What's more, she didn't care.

She heard footsteps then, and the bedroom door opening. She looked up to see Tony standing at the foot of the bed. He was wearing a dark cotton robe and looked freshly shaven.

'Come on, sleepyhead,' he said, reaching down to grab her toe. 'Let's go for a swim.'

'What time is it?' Diana murmured sleepily.

'Almost eight.'

She groaned and rolled over on her side. 'Oh, no. It's too early.' Then she remembered. 'Besides, Leia and Tomo are due any minute.'

'I just sent them home,' he said smugly. 'Come on, get up! We've got the place to ourselves today.'

'Later,' she mumbled, and burrowed her head deeper into the pillow.

Then suddenly she felt the sheet being snatched away, and sat up in bed abruptly. 'Tony!' she cried. 'What are you doing?'

'I'm asserting my masculinity,' he said.

As she watched, wide-eyed, he came to the side of the bed, shed his robe, then scooped her up in his arms. She started laughing, then, and pounding on his chest in protest as he strode out of the bedroom and headed for the lanai.

'Put me down, you idiot!' she choked out. 'You'll hurt yourself. You don't have to prove your masculinity to me, for heaven's sake.'

Then, as he went through the doorway and marched purposefully towards the shimmering blue swimmming-pool, she stiffened in his arms. 'Tony, you wouldn't!' she cried in alarm. 'Tony, I don't even have a bathing-suit on.'

He was at the very edge of the pool now. 'What in the world do you need a bathing-suit for?' he asked calmly, and let her go.

The next thing she knew, she was spluttering in the water. She scrambled upwards, fuming, until she broke the surface. Tossing her wet hair out of her eyes and gasping for breath, she glared up at him.

'You *beast*!' she shouted when she saw the self-satisfied smirk on his face.

But when the smirk turned soft and her eyes travelled over his tall straight figure, splendid in its nakedness, its sheer maleness, her annoyance vanished. He raised his arms, then, and dived cleanly into the water.

He traversed the width of the pool under the surface, like a sleek brown fish, then came up behind her and put his arms around her, cupping her breasts in his hands. After a moment, he turned her around and grinned down at her.

'Are you angry?' he asked.

How could she be? Wasn't this what she had prayed for, dreamed of, ever since she'd come to the island? She'd been terrified that this carefree, playful side of Tony's nature had been so damaged by what he had had to endure in prison, perhaps killed for ever, that she felt as though she'd just been handed a precious gift.

'Yes, I am,' she said aloud with mock severity. 'Asserting your masculinity, indeed! You should be ashamed of yourself. You almost drowned me.'

'You swim like a fish,' he snorted.

She tossed her head and eyed him menacingly. 'I'll get even,' she warned. 'When you least expect it, you know what I'll do with your precious masculinity.'

'Mm,' he said. 'I know what I hope you'll do.' He rubbed against her, eyeing her wickedly. 'I can hardly wait!' He laughed and swam away from her. 'Come on—twenty laps, then we'll have breakfast.'

'Ten laps,' she amended firmly, swimming after him. 'Then I'll go and cook breakfast.'

All in all, Diana thought late that afternoon, it was a perfect day, at least the happiest day she could ever remember having in her life. She was lying out on the lanai on the chaise-longue, watching Tony's retreating figure as he jogged up the beach.

The change in him from one day to the next had been astonishing. It was like a dam that had burst, or a log-jam coming unstuck at last. From the remote, silent man of yesterday, he had become a laughing highly potent lover. The power of love could indeed work miracles, she mused thoughtfully. It occured to her, too, that perhaps Dan's appearance might have had something to do with it. Had it made Tony just a little jealous to see their easy, casual affection for each other?

After their early morning swim, they had showered together, which, of course, led to some interesting experimentation in the tiled stall and left them both helpless with laughter. Diana had finally talked Tony into putting on some clothes, but only when she promised to wear nothing underneath the loose cotton shift.

'I like to look at you,' he'd said. 'I've been without the sight of you for so long that I can't get enough of just looking.'

Well, she'd thought, she liked to look at him, too. It had been just as long for her, and the obvious delight he took in her body filled her with joy. But still, she'd told him, they weren't exactly marooned on a desert island. Someone might stop by. Besides, she'd added, looking always seemed to lead to touching, and they couldn't spend all their time in bed.

Tony was coming towards the house now in an easy, loping stride, and she was struck with admiration at the sight of his lean athletic body, the grace of his movements and the way his muscles tautened and rippled as he ran.

When he reached the lanai, panting from his exertions, he leaned over the chaise to kiss her. His skin glistened with perspiration, and his damp black hair fell over his forehead. His skin smelled clean and earthy, a heady combination.

'How about another swim?' he suggested, reaching down to unfasten the shorts he was wearing.

'No, thanks,' she replied drily. 'You go ahead. I'll go and fix us a drink.' She glanced up at the sky. 'The sun is over the yard-arm, isn't it?'

She went into the kitchen to mix their drinks, and when she reached in the refrigerator for the tonic water, she wondered if she shouldn't be thinking about fixing something for their dinner. Leia usually took care of that, but Tony had sent her home as soon as she'd arrived that morning.

Smiling at the remembrance, she began going through the cupboards for an inspiration. Perhaps just a salad, she thought. There was lots of fresh fruit, an uncut pineapple, mangoes, papayas. She could make biscuits or muffins, or maybe drive into town to the bakery for croissants.

'Hey, where's my drink?' Tony called. He appeared at the door of the kitchen, a towel around his shoulders and his tan shorts back on.

'Sorry,' she said. 'I was wondering what to do about dinner.'

Just then the telephone rang, a very rare occurence. There was an extension on the kitchen counter. Diana glanced at Tony. He had gone quite still, and the smile was replaced by the hint of a frown. It rang again.

'Better answer it,' he said at last.

It was Janet Patterson. 'Oh, hi, Janet,' said Diana. 'How are you?'

Although she was closer to her mother's age than hers, Diana had always felt a strong rapport with the slender, grey-haired woman whom she had known virtually all her life. She was more modern in her views, and less indoctrinated by the stiff-upper-lip, duty-above-all military code that dominated her mother's life. She knew everybody, and her parties were legend.

'We're fine,' said Janet. 'A houseful of people, as usual, but that's the way I like it. I think you know most of them.'

While she rattled off several familiar names, Diana saw Tony go over to the sink and finish making the drinks she had started. He came back and handed her one, then sat down across the counter from her on one of the high metal stools and watched her.

'Well, anyway,' Janet went on, 'we all got our heads together last night and decided to drive into the big hotel in Lihue on Saturday night to try their big *luau*. We'd like to have you and Tony join us.'

'I don't know, Janet. We're living pretty quietly these days.'

'How is he?'

'Oh, he's fine. Quite back to his old self.' Diana gave him a suggestive leer, and he almost choked on his drink.

'You'll have to admit, Diana,' Janet said, 'that we've all been very good and practised a lot of restraint leaving you two alone for so long to enjoy your second honeymoon. But don't you think it's about time you got back into the swing of things? Dan says Tony looks great. You can't keep him all to yourself for ever.'

'When is it again, Janet? Saturday?'

She put her hand over the mouthpiece of the telephone and whispered the word '*luau*' to Tony. Immediately, he frowned and shook his head.

'Right,' Janet said. 'You could come to our place first and have a drink, then we'd all go on together.'

'I think we'd better pass on this one, Janet. Maybe next time.' She was rewarded by a grateful look from Tony.

'Well, all right. But I'm not going to give up.'

'Good! I'm glad,' Diana replied with a little laugh. 'We'll get together soon. Thanks for calling, Janet, and give everyone my love.'

When she had hung up, Tony came around the counter and took her in his arms. He held her tenderly for several moments, his face buried in her hair, his body hard and strong against her. He put his hand underneath her hair and gently kneaded the back of her neck. There was no passion in his embrace, but she could feel waves of warmth emanating from him.

He cupped her chin in his hand and tilted her head back so that she was looking up at his face. What she saw there made her glow with pleasure. For the first time, the light in his brown eyes was one of pure love.

'You wanted to go, didn't you?' he asked softly.

Diana tightened her arms around his waist. 'I'd rather be here with you.'

'But you did want to go.'

She shrugged and cocked her head to one side, smiling up at him. 'Maybe. But only to show off my handsome new husband.'

She couldn't resist raising her hand to run a finger over his mouth. 'I love your mouth,' she murmured, as she traced first the chiselled outline of the narrow upper lip, then the full lower one. He opened his mouth and bit gently on the exploring finger.

'And I love you,' Tony said, holding her gaze in his. 'And I'm very grateful you turned the Pattersons down. It's selfish, I guess, but I want you all to myself, at least for a little while longer.'

It was what she wanted too, Diana thought, slumping against him. She closed her eyes and laid her head on his heart as he stroked her back. She had been a little disappointed to miss the party on Saturday night, but there would be other parties, and it was well worth it to have elicited that declaration of love from Tony. Until then, she hadn't been quite sure that he did really love her, really trust her. Now she knew at last that he did, and that was all she needed.

Diana floated through the next two weeks on a cloud of euphoria. Their lovemaking continued to be perfect. It was totally spontaneous, too. They were quite circumspect while Tomo and Leia were there, but as soon as the couple left, they would make love whenever and wherever they pleased.

One night, just after sunset, Tony even coaxed her down to the beach to swim naked. Once she overcame her initial apprehension and realised that they truly were private there, she enjoyed the experience more than she ever would have dreamed possible.

The house was built on a small sheltered bay where the surf was not nearly so overpowering as it was on the more open stretches of beach, and once they got past the breaking waves, the water was quite calm, and so clear that Diana could see the flat stones on the bottom, even, occasionally, a colourful fish darting by.

It was intensely invigorating to be carried on the buoyant salt water, still warm from the sun's rays, and she floated mindlessly, her long dark hair spread out around her, secure in the knowledge that Tony was nearby. He liked to swim out a little farther, but was never gone for long, and she always knew when he came back by the touch of his lips on her breast or the feel of his hands on her thighs. They would swim silently together to the shore, then, both of them filled with barely-contained excitement, make love on the damp packed sand of the beach.

Only one thing marred those halcyon days, and that was a nagging worry at the back of Diana's mind about the future. Tony was perfectly fit now in every way, mentally and physically. Only occasionally now did she surprise the old haunted look in his eyes when he didn't know she was watching him, and the look of suffering was always transformed into a warm smile of welcome the moment he saw her.

She realised that he would probably always have to deal with those ghosts from the past, but she hoped in time that the scars would fade as surely as the welts on his back.

Tony never spoke to her about his experiences in prison. Once or twice she broached the subject, but his face always closed up when she did. His eyes would go blank, his mouth become set in a rigid line, and he would simply vanish from her mentally. She would panic, then, terrified of losing him, of being shut out again, and would change the subject immediately or go to sit on his lap, twining her arms around his neck and holding his dark head fiercely, protectively, to her breast.

Finally, she learned to accept the fact that he intended to deal with his past alone, and she decided never to mention it again. He never asked her about her life during the seven years they were apart, after all, and in the end she came to believe it was probably better that way.

That still left the future, however, a future they would share, and on that subject she felt she did have some rights. He still shut himself up in his room every day after his morning workout, speaking in vague terms of the possibility of writing a book some day.

One night, then, Diana decided it was time to tackle him about his plans. There had been a heavy tropical downpour earlier that afternoon, and it had rained steadily since then. It was the first time in the weeks they had been on Kauai that they hadn't been able to go outdoors, and by the time she'd cleaned up the kitchen after their evening meal, Diana was feeling restless and bored from being cooped up all day.

Tony was in the living-room reading when she carried in their after-dinner coffee. It's all right for him, she thought, a little resentfully, setting the tray down on the table in front of him. He has his books, his work. I can't even take care of my own house, with Leia shooing me away every time I try.

When he looked up from his book and smiled at her, however, her momentary resentment faded instantly.

NO COST! NO OBLIGATION!
NO PURCHASE NECESSARY!

PLAY "LUCKY 7"
AND GET AS MANY AS SIX FREE GIFTS...

HOW TO PLAY:

1. With a coin, carefully scratch off the three silver boxes at the right. This makes you eligible to receive one or more free books, and possibly other gifts, depending on what is revealed beneath the scratch-off area.

2. You'll receive brand-new Harlequin Presents® novels, never before published. When you return this card, we'll send you the books and gifts you qualify for *absolutely free!*

3. And, a month later, we'll send you 8 additional novels to read and enjoy. If you decide to keep them, you'll pay only $1.99 per book, a savings of 26¢ per book. And $1.99 per book is all you pay. There is no charge for shipping and handling. There are no hidden extras.

4. We'll also send you additional free gifts from time to time, as well as our newsletter.

5. You must be completely satisfied, or you may return a shipment of books and cancel at any time.

FOLDING UMBRELLA FREE

This bright burgundy umbrella is made of durable nylon. It folds to a compact 15″ to fit into your bag or briefcase. And it could be YOURS FREE when you play "LUCKY 7."

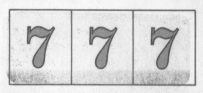

PLAY "LUCKY 7"

Just scratch off the three silver boxes.
Then check below to see which gifts you get.

YES! I have scratched off the silver boxes. Please send me all the gifts for which I qualify. I understand I am under no obligation to purchase any books, as explained on the opposite page.

108 CIP CAMK

NAME

ADDRESS   APT.

CITY   STATE   ZIP

7	7	7	WORTH FOUR FREE BOOKS, FREE UMBRELLA AND FREE SURPRISE GIFT
🍒	🍒	🍒	WORTH FOUR FREE BOOKS AND FREE UMBRELLA
●	●	●	WORTH FOUR FREE BOOKS
🔔	🔔	🍒	WORTH TWO FREE BOOKS

He was so dear, so loving, all she could hope for in a husband, and she knew how lucky she was.

'I've been thinking, Tony,' Diana said carefully as she poured out the coffee.

'You'd better watch that,' he warned, taking the cup from her. 'It's a dangerous occupation.'

She frowned at the patronising tone. 'I'm serious.'

'Sorry, darling,' he said quickly. 'Tell me about it.'

'Shouldn't we be planning some kind of future?' she asked. 'I mean, we can't stay here for ever. Surely you've given some thought to what you want to do, where you want to live. I was hoping . . .' She broke off. She didn't want to push him. Still, it was her future, too. Didn't she have some say in it? She looked at him. He was gazing at her thoughtfully.

'Go on,' he prompted. 'What were you hoping? I really want to hear.'

'Well then, I was hoping you'd decide to do what Arne Jacobson asked you to do.'

'You mean, go back on active duty?'

She nodded. Tony looked away, then, staring into space, not saying anything for a long time.

'I haven't decided about that,' he said at last. 'Frankly, it doesn't appeal much to me at the moment. Somehow I seem to have lost my old military fervour.' He shook his head. 'I don't know, Diana. Is that really what you want?'

'Well,' she said slowly, 'I do like the life. After all, it's the only life I've ever known. What else would you do?'

He set his cup down on the table, then turned to her. 'I could teach, I suppose. Arne did mention that he could probably get me a spot at the Naval Academy in Annapolis.'

That might not be so bad, she thought. It would mean no more travelling, but Annapolis was a lovely town, and she'd heard that the social life was active. Maryland was close to Washington, New York, Philadelphia, even Boston. It might be fun, at least for a while.

'I think that's a very good idea,' she said with enthusiasm. 'You could probably find the time to work on your book, too, if you were teaching, and there would be plenty for me to do. It *is* a naval installation.'

'Yes,' he agreed. 'It would have definite advantages.' Then he laughed a little diffidently. 'Shall I tell you my pipe-dream, my castle in the air?'

Diana smiled. 'Please do.'

'I have this constantly recurring fantasy about finding a small house on the water up in the San Juan Islands, settling in there, writing my book, raising a family.'

Tony was watching her very closely as he spoke. She continued to smile brightly, but underneath, her heart plummeted sickeningly. The San Juan Islands! That remote, isolated place far up in the waters between Canada and northern Washington state! Settling in there! Raising a family!

The muscles of her rigid jaw began to ache and she could hold the fake smile no longer. She gave him a stricken look.

'You hate the idea,' he said flatly. 'I was afraid of that.'

'Tony,' she faltered, 'I don't know what to say. It just never occurred to me that you'd want to bury yourself in an isolated place like the San Juans.'

'It's not the Arctic Circle,' he said drily. 'The islands are fairly well populated. Quite a few people actually live there.'

'But what would I do?' she wailed. 'I wouldn't know

anybody. There can't be any night-life. All my friends are Navy people.'

'You'd make new friends, and we'd probably start a family right away. You do want children, don't you, Diana?'

'Well, yes, I suppose so, some day. But not yet. It's too soon.'

'Diana, you're twenty-seven years old. I'm thirty-five. That's hardly too soon to start having children.'

She laughed shakily. '*Start* having children? You talk as though you want several!'

He shrugged. 'Children are very important to me. Like you, I never thought much about them before, but those years in prison changed all that. Children *are* the future, our link with it, our legacy to it. –'

She could only stare at him. He could be speaking a foreign language for all she understood what he was saying to her. Her head whirled. She could feel his eyes still on her, waiting for her to respond.

But what could she say? He'd taken her completely by surprise. Surely he wasn't serious? He'd said it was a pipe-dream, a castle in the air. He couldn't possibly expect her to give up her friends, her pleasant way of life, and go traipsing off after him to a cold northern island and spend the rest of her life raising a houseful of children while he wrote books. It was unthinkable!

No, she thought, of course he wasn't serious. It was only a fantasy, after all. He'd said it himself. She would persuade him to take the teaching position at Annapolis. That would be an ideal compromise. Tony was a fair man, and he loved her. He'd want her to be happy.

We've been isolated for too long, she thought. It's not healthy. What we need is to get out more, be with people, renew our old friendships, develop a social life. She turned to him, calmer now that she had made her decision.

'Janet Patterson called again this morning,' she said. She saw his face fall, the hint of disappointment in his eyes, and rushed on, 'That *luau* at the hotel in Lihue two weeks ago turned out so well that they've decided to have one catered at their place. Would you like to go?'

'You miss all that, don't you, Diana?' Tony asked quietly.

She raised her chin. 'Yes. Yes, I do miss it.' Then her gaze softened and she reached for his hand, cradling it against her cheek. 'Tony, I love you so much. You know that. These past weeks alone here with you have been heaven. But try to understand. You have your work—I have nothing.'

He pulled her to him then and held her in his arms, stroking her hair and murmuring in her ear. 'I do understand, darling. I've been very selfish. I'm sorry.' He raised her face in his hands and kissed her on the tip of her nose. 'Of course we'll go to the *luau* at the Pattersons'. It sounds like fun.'

CHAPTER SIX

ON Saturday night, Diana sat at the dressing-table in her bedroom getting ready to go to the Pattersons' *luau*. Even though Tony slept in her bed every night, they still maintained separate bedrooms so that Tony could use his for a study.

It would be their first appearance in public together, and she was a little nervous about it. Ever since their talk a few nights ago, Tony had seemed slightly more withdrawn, as though he were making an effort to be cheerful and attentive. His attitude towards her was not quite as carefree and spontaneous as it had been before he'd agreed to go to the party.

It could just be my imagination, she thought, brushing out her long dark hair. Perhaps I'm feeling a little guilty for forcing him into something he really didn't want to do. But that was silly, she decided. He surely realised himself that eventually he'd have to get back into the real world. He would know everyone there. After the first few awkward moments had passed, he'd feel right at home. Once he got reacquainted with his old friends, he would enjoy himself. And, she added, she just hoped give up his crazy scheme to bury himself in some remote island retreat.

He hadn't mentioned that castle in the air again, and she hoped the whole subject would just go away. After that last unpleasant discussion, neither of them had reopened the question of their future.

101

Diana gave her reflection in the mirror one last appraising glance. She really did look her best, she decided, better than she'd looked in years. Her skin was tanned to a deep golden brown, emphasising the clear whites around her green eyes and the pale yellow of her dress. She wasn't too sure about the dress, though.

She frowned at the low scooped neckline, then twisted a little on the bench and leaned forward to judge just how revealing it was. To please Tony, she had abandoned all her bras, but maybe for a public appearance she should add that little extra bit of protection.

She heard him come up behind her then, and saw his image in the mirror. He was standing quite still with his eyes fastened on her own reflection.

'Yum, yum,' he said with a smile. The brown eyes gleamed. 'You look good enough to eat.' He leaned down and pressed his lips to her bare back.

'I don't know, Tony,' she said, still fussing with the neckline of the dress. 'What do you think? Is it a little too suggestive?'

He put his hands on her shoulders. 'Sit still for a minute and let me look.' He held her firmly so she wouldn't move and gazed thoughtfully into the mirror for several moments.

'Well,' he said judiciously, 'I know what it suggests to me. I think a more thorough investigation might be in order, though, before I make a definite decision.'

The hands on her shoulders slid down over her throat and upper chest until they settled firmly, one on each breast. With a little sigh of pleasure, she leaned back against him and watched the large brown hands as they moulded the high, soft fullness in a hypnotic, highly sensual rhythm.

Their gaze met in the mirror. Her lips parted when she saw his eyes darkening with desire. They were half-closed now, the long lashes fluttering against his high cheekbones. He slid one hand beneath the low neckline of the yellow dress and when his fingers began to play lightly with the already hard nipple of her bare breast, a hot rush of desire started in her loins and spread quickly to warm her whole body.

'Tony,' she said weakly, putting her hand over his, 'we've got to go.'

With a long sigh of regret, he withdrew his exploring hand slowly, lingering and drawing it out as long as possible.

'You're a hard woman, Mrs Hamilton,' he said. 'But to answer your question, you look perfect. Just don't bend over too far in front of any of the other men!'

She turned on the bench. 'You don't look so bad yourself, my friend,' she said, eyeing him with appreciation. He had on tan slacks and a light cocoa-coloured knitted shirt which fitted him to perfection now that his muscle structure had regained its full strength. His dark hair shone, and the white teeth flashed in the old familiar broad grin she loved so well.

'Well then,' he said, 'since we agree we're both presentable and fit for polite society, shall we go?'

The party was already in full swing when they arrived at the Pattersons', less than half an hour later. As they drove down the curved pavement that meandered through the lush tropical garden in front, they could already hear the music coming from behind the house.

'Sounds like live music,' Tony remarked, pulling up behind a row of parked cars.

'Oh, trust Janet Patterson to do it up right,' said Diana. 'No gramophone records for her when she can get the real thing!'

They got out of the car and started walking around the side of the house towards the beach at the back, following the loud strains of steel guitars and native drums pounding out a rhythmic, fast-paced Hawaiian tune.

The huge lanai was filled with people. The sun had set, and it was beginning to grow dark, but the air was still mild and balmy, with a soft breeze blowing off the ocean in the background. A bar was set up near the house, manned by two native men in white jackets.

At the far end of the paved lanai, near the beach, an enormous low table was set up, with cushions on the ground around it on every side. Nearby a pit had been dug to make a Hawaiian oven, with a whole pig turning slowly on a spit over the hot coals glowing on the bottom. Japanese lanterns had been strung over the whole area and were twinkling colourfully now in the gathering dusk.

Janet Patterson spotted them first, and with a little shriek of delight, detached herself from the crowd, a drink in her hand, and came rushing towards them.

'Tony Hamilton!' she cried.

It seemed to Diana that every head in the place immediately swivelled towards them. She could feel Tony tense up beside her, his body go slightly rigid, and his hand clench hers a little tighter.

As Janet threw her arms around him and kissed him affectionately on the cheek, the crowd began to surge towards them, converging to surround them in an informal circle. George Patterson came forward and extended a hand to Tony, clapping him on the shoulder with the other one.

'By God, it really is you!' he said with feeling. 'If you aren't a sight for sore eyes!' As they shook hands, he beamed on Tony with a proprietorial air, as though he'd just invented him out of thin air himself.

It was sheer bedlam from then on. Almost everybody there had at least a nodding acquaintance with Tony, and all of them were anxious to greet the hero who had so miraculously been returned from the dead.

Diana stood back from the crowd, watching Tony anxiously to gauge his reaction to all the fuss being made over him. It was inevitable, she thought philosophically, something he'd just have to suffer through, at least once. He seemed all right. He was smiling easily, speaking with everyone and looking so tall and handsome, by far the best-looking man there. She heaved a sigh of relief. It really was going to be all right.

'You look as though you could use a drink,' came a voice at her elbow, and she turned to see Dan Armstrong, looking fit and tanned and rather handsome himself. She gave him a warm smile of welcome.

'Dan! It's good to see you. I was afraid you'd be gone by now.'

'The Pattersons prevailed on me to stick around a while longer,' he told her, leading her towards the bar. 'Besides, I was hoping to get in a good visit with Tony before I left. How is he? He looks marvellous, brimming with health and vigour.'

'He's wonderful,' she replied. 'Perfectly fit and all recovered.'

'And you? You look pretty fetching yourself. And pretty smug, I might add, just like the cat that swallowed the canary.'

'Oh, Dan,' she said, putting a hand on his arm, 'I'm so happy. It's just like it used to be.' She laughed happily. 'No. It's better.'

'I can see that,' he said a lttle grimly. Then he smiled. 'I'm glad, Diana, really I am. I'm glad it's Tony who put those stars in your eyes. If I can't have you, I'd rather it were him than anyone else.' He turned to the bartender. 'Two gin and tonics.'

For the next hour or so, Diana found herself less and less concerned with how Tony was reacting to his first venture into society after his long imprisonment, illness and recuperation, and more and more simply enjoying herself with her old friends. Occasionally, their eyes would meet over a distance, and they would exchange a brief, warm smile, but he seemed quite content to mingle with the others, moving easily from one group to another.

When it was time to eat, the thirty or so guests were seated at the long low table, which was loaded with huge platters of the roast pig, Hawaiian yams wrapped in taro leaves and trays of fresh fruit, all set out amid bowls of tropical flowers.

They had all been given colourful leis to wear around their necks, and the women orchids, gardenias or hibiscus to pin in their hair. It was growing darker now, and the tall palms that lined the edge of the beach loomed black against the deep blue sky, swaying gently in the evening breeze.

The Pattersons had set up a small platform some feet away from the far end of the table, where the small band was now playing soft romantic songs of the islands. To their right, two native girls in colourful cotton bandeaux and swirling grass skirts performed a graceful hula.

'It's a wonderful party, Janet,' Diana said to her hostess, who was sitting on her right. Dan was at her left, and Tony was across the table and down a few seats.

'It seems to be going well,' Janet replied. 'You never know until it actually gets under way. Some of my worst flops were parties I was certain would be a huge success.'

'Well, you can't miss on this one.' Diana waved her hand in an all-encompassing gesture. 'The food, the music, the setting, the people. It's all perfect.'

Janet gave her a rather amused look. 'You're so high up on your fleecy cloud that I think you'd be happy with bread and water on a desert island, so long as it was with Tony!'

Diana smiled and lowered her eyes. 'Am I that obvious?'

Janet laughed. 'Don't apologise. I think it's great. He looks terrific,' she added, with a nod in Tony's direction. 'He always was a handsome man, but now he's—oh, how shall I put it?—*interesting*, I guess is the word. Rather mysterious, like a man with a dangerous past.'

'He had an awful time of it,' Diana said soberly.

'Does he talk about it much?'

'No. He just wants to put it behind him.'

Someone called to her from across the table. 'Say, Diana, I was just telling Tony about that New Year's Eve when we all left the Sand Point Officers' Club at midnight and drove out to Shilshole Bay to walk on the beach.' It was Pam Madison, and she was just a little drunk. 'Remember?' she went on, waving her glass in the air. 'You lost your shoes and Dan had to spend two hours out there with a flashlight looking for them.'

Diana laughed and turned to Dan, at her side. 'It was *not* two hours,' she protested. 'As I remember, they were right under that bush where I kept telling him I'd left them.'

This brought about a general howl of laughter, and raised a spate of similar reminiscences. The Hallowe'en they'd gone on a scavenger hunt and Dan and Diana had won first prize by turning up with a freshly-dug carrot from a neighbour's vegetable garden; the Easter they'd had the egg hunt in Volunteer Park and Diana and Dan had almost won first prize until she'd dropped all their eggs into the fishpond.

After about twenty minutes of this, it began to dawn on Diana that in almost every hilarious story, she was paired with Dan. It was a natural thing to do, she thought. Although she'd gone out with several different men throughout the years of her "widowhood", it was Dan who had been the old standby. As Tony's best friend, he had been at her side at the military funeral, and from the beginning he had assumed a protective role in her life that she had simply taken for granted.

Still, it did sound bad, as though they were an old married couple, or at least conducting a long-term affair, the way they were linked together so naturally in the minds of their friends.

She glanced at Tony out of the corner of her eye to see how he was taking it. He had never quizzed her about those years she had been alone. He wanted to forget both their pasts, to make an entirely fresh start. Maybe later tonight she should tell him that there had never been anything more between herself and Dan than casual affection. It might reassure him, just in case these references to shared experiences bothered him.

He seemed all right. He was leaning forward, his elbows propped on the table, his chin on the backs of his hands, silently listening to the banter going on around him, a half-smile on his lips. Was the smile a little forced? she wondered, and she mentally reaffirmed her decision to discuss it with him when they got home.

Nothing can come between us now, she vowed silently, fiercely. A great wave of love for Tony rose up in her. She tried to catch his eye, but his head was turned now towards George Patterson, who sat at the foot of the table. He was also a little drunk, she noticed, and was speaking in a loud voice.

'So, Tony, what are your plans? Are you going to take a medical disability? Retire early, as I did?'

Tony leaned back in his chair. 'I can hardly do that, George,' he said equably, 'since I don't have a physical handicap.'

George waved a hand in the air, spilling a good part of his drink in the process. 'Oh, those things can be arranged if you know the right people. What, then? Going back on active status?'

Over the hum of conversation going on around her, Diana perked up her ears. They had come to no definite decision about the future, hadn't even discussed it since the impasse they'd reached a few nights ago, and she was anxious to hear his reply.

'I really haven't made any definite plans yet, George,' she heard him say. 'It will depend a lot on what the Navy wants me to do, I guess.' He smiled crookedly. 'Their version of active duty and mine might be two different things.'

'In other words,' said George, slurring his words and

leering knowingly, 'no more spying missions.'

There was a sudden hush in the murmur of voices at the table as all eyes shifted to stare at the two men. Diana could cheerfully have murdered George. Of all subjects to bring up at a party, he had to choose the one thing Tony didn't want to discuss. She gave him an uneasy glance, apprehensive about his reaction.

She saw him take a long swallow of his drink. Then, his expression impassive, he said, 'It wasn't a spying mission, George. I just strayed off course.' His tone was light and casual, but Diana recognised the hard, withdrawn look as the brown eyes glazed over.

'Ho, ho!' spluttered George. 'You were the best pilot I ever saw. You couldn't stray off course if you tried.'

Beside her, Diana felt Janet rise abruptly to her feet. 'If everyone is through eating,' she said in a loud cheerful voice, 'let's go back on the lanai and dance. We could all use the exercise, I'm sure, after that enormous meal!'

Blessing Janet for her tact and good sense, Diana got up and started to make her way around the table to Tony, but before she could reach him, another group of people had clustered around him. She sighed with frustration as she watched them converge and close ranks. Then Dan asked her to dance, and for the rest of the evening there wasn't one moment where she could find Tony alone. All the women wanted to dance with him, and all the men wanted to talk to him. Finally she decided she might as well enjoy herself. They could talk in private when they got home.

The party didn't break up until two o'clock in the morning, and when she and Tony got to the car, she was surprised when he asked her if she minded driving home.

'I shouldn't really be driving at all,' he said

apologetically. 'Not without a licence. Another little item I'll have to see to soon.'

The driveway was well lit, and Diana gave him a closer look. He was exhausted, she realised when she saw the old haggard look back on his face. They shouldn't have stayed so long on their first outing. She was about to say something sympathetic, but the set expression on his face told her it would be a mistake.

Instead, she only murmured, 'Of course,' and got in the car on the driver's side.

On the way home they didn't speak. As soon as she started the car, Tony put his head back on the headrest and closed his eyes. Diana darted an occasional glance at him as she drove, but knew it was best not to say anything to him just yet.

Was he just tired, she wondered as she pulled into their own driveway, or was he upset over George's remarks? Finally, she made up her mind she would just ask him, tired or not. She parked the car in front of the house, shut off the engine and turned to him.

'Here we are,' she said. 'Home at last.' Tony opened his eyes and shifted to an upright position. 'Tired, darling?' she asked.

'A little.'

'We probably overdid our first night out.'

'Probably.'

He hadn't looked at her once, and his curt replies were not very conducive to the conversation she'd hoped to have with him. Without another word, they got out of the car and started walking towards the house.

When they got inside, Diana decided she would have to try once more. His silence was beginning to frighten her a little. Their close intimacy of the past fortnight had been like heaven to her, and she was terrified of losing it. He seemed to be retreating from her back to the place he was when she first saw him in the hospital.

I've got to be calm, she thought. They were near the door to the kitchen now, and when she switched on the light, the expression she saw on his face was so distant, so absorbed, that he could have been a million miles away. I've got to reach him, she thought in a panic. Her throat felt dry and raspy, and she cleared it before she spoke.

'Are you hungry?' she asked in a casual tone.

Tony turned to her then, a look of mild surprise on his face, as though she had disturbed his concentration. Then, to her vast relief, he smiled.

'No,' he said. 'Not after that feed.' He hesitated. 'I am a little tired, though. Think I'll head right for bed, if you don't mind.'

'No, of course I don't mind.' Diana laughed nervously. 'We shouldn't have stayed so long.'

'Oh, I imagine I'll get used to it in time. I'm just a little out of practice. Well, I'll say goodnight, then,' he said, and turned away from her.

It was all right, she thought, watching him go. He was only tired, that was all. Still, she had to make sure.

'Tony!' she called to him. He turned around. 'Tony, did anything happen tonight to disturb you?' She shrugged and spread her hands. 'I mean, George and his stupid probing.' No point mentioning the way the others had paired her off with Dan, she decided. If it bothered him, surely he'd tell her.

'Oh, lord, no,' he replied. 'George was a little drunk. No harm done. I'm just a little tired, that's all,' he added, and she couldn't miss the slight note of impatience in his voice.

'Okay,' she said, going up to him. They were in the hall now, near the bedrooms. 'If you're sure.'

Tony smiled and kissed her lightly on the forehead. 'I'm sure.'

He turned from her then and went into his own bedroom. She stood out in the hallway for several moments, somewhat reassured, but still vaguely anxious. It wasn't until she'd turned out the lights and gone into her own room that she realised why. For the first time since they'd embarked on their second honeymoon, they would be sleeping apart.

After that night of the Pattersons' party, there began a change in their relationship. The symptoms of it were so subtle that although Diana was vaguely aware that something was different, she didn't quite know how to halt its momentum or even if she should try.

Perhaps this was what happened to all married couples, she thought one morning two weeks later. Once they left the solitary life to become part of a larger society in the real world, the intensity of the relationship was bound to diminish. It was only normal.

She was still in bed at nine-thirty, awakened by the clatter of typewriter keys coming from Tony's room next door. She had a slight headache. They had gone to another party last night and had come home quite late.

She lay there with her eyes closed, still half asleep, thinking over the events of the past few weeks. The party at the Pattersons' seemed to have unlocked a door that brought the outside world into the private paradise they had known before. She regretted this in a way. There was no more of the spontaneous lovemaking she had enjoyed so much, no more nude evening swims in the moonlight.

Was it really just settling into a more normal married life, she wondered, or was it something more than that? There seemed to be a barrier between them now, even when they were alone, a barrier that was growing higher every day. Was that really what happened in a good marriage? Shouldn't they be growing closer instead of drifting farther apart?

While their social life had expanded dramatically, Tony stuck religiously to the daily routine he had devised for himself. He still rose early in the morning for his workout and swim, and after a large breakfast, he went directly to his room to work, so that they didn't see each other at all until later in the day, sometimes not until dinner, if Diana had somewhere to go in the afternoon. There always seemed to be something to do now, luncheons, tennis games, excursions into Honolulu to go shopping, but Tony never went along.

He had even begun to beg off the evening affairs, and she found herself thrown more and more with Dan as her escort. She didn't really object to this. She liked Dan, and he enjoyed the whirl of social activity as much as she did. She would just rather it was Tony.

She wondered, too, if she was doing something wrong. Wouldn't it be better to give up her friends and try to share Tony's life more? But how could she, when he shut her out the way he did? What would she do with herself all day while he was working on his book?

Still pondering, she got out of bed and went into the bathroom. He used not to shut me out, though, she thought as she soaped herself under the shower. We were getting closer all the time. He was really beginning to open up to me. Why did he stop? What made him back away like that, just when it all seemed to be working out so well?

It was after ten o'clock by now. She just had time for a light breakfast, then at eleven thirty, Janet Patterson was coming to pick her up to drive into Lihue for a luncheon in honour of the Madisons, who were returning home at the end of the week. Soon it would be March, almost the end of winter. Seattle's climate would improve soon, and little by little her friends were leaving the islands.

Diana dressed carefully in a well-fitting white linen dress she had bought on her last shopping trip into Honolulu, then brushed out her hair and put on a dash of pale lipstick. It was all the make-up she needed, she decided, with her heavy tan. She had just surveyed her reflection in the mirror for the last time when there came a light knock on the door and Tony walked in.

'Good morning,' he said with a smile. 'You look ravishing. Is that new dress for my benefit?'

'Hardly,' she said, giving him a wry look. 'I never see you during the day.'

For some reason, his question had irritated her. He looked very appealing in his brief shorts and white knitted shirt. His long legs and arms had regained their muscular strength and were bronzed to a toasty brown by the sun. The smile on his sensuous mouth was extremely enticing, and the look of appreciation in his brown eyes warmed her. Why, then, did she suddenly feel so angry with him?

She noticed the way his smile had faded at her sharp retort and turned back to the mirror to fasten her earrings. Tears pricked at her eyes. What had made her say a thing like that when what she'd wanted to do was run to him, kiss that wonderful mouth, and feel those arms around her, holding her close.

There was a long silence, and she could sense him hesitating at the door. When he spoke, his voice was flat.

'I take it you're going out.'

She whirled around to face him. 'Yes. You were invited, if you recall, but, as usual, you chose not to go.'

He ran a hand through his dark hair and gave her a troubled look. 'Diana, I've tried to explain it to you. If I'm going to get this book written, I have to discipline myself, stick to a rule. A rule that's broken even once is no longer a rule. Can't you try to understand?'

'Yes,' she said, nodding vigorously, 'I understand that part. What I don't understand is why you need to bury yourself when you've got a perfectly good job with the Navy waiting for you.'

They had avoided all discussion of Captain Jacobson's offer of a teaching job at Annapolis. Now it was out in the open at last. Tony was staring out of the window, looking very unhappy, she thought, and her heart went out to him. But she had to stand her ground.

'Actually,' he said at last, 'that's what I wanted to speak to you about.' He shifted his gaze to her. 'Arne called a few nights ago to tell me the offer was still open.'

'I see.' Diana drew in a deep breath and waited. Tony walked over to the window and stood staring out at the beach, his hands shoved in the back pockets of his shorts.

'He wanted a decision. They have to fill the spot right away,' he said in a muffled voice.

'What did you tell him?' She stood there staring at his back, her whole body rigid, hardly able to breathe from the choking sensation in her throat, waiting to hear him speak.

Finally, he turned around to face her. 'I turned him down.'

It felt to Diana that all the breath had suddenly been knocked out of her. She felt physically ill. A host of conflicting emotions assailed her, a deep sense of dread and despair, but most of all, a rising, uncontrollable anger. She clenched her fists at her sides and glared at him, half blind with fury.

'How dare you!' she said in a low voice, trembling with feeling. 'How could you do such a thing without consulting me? You had no right!'

He raised a hand in a helpless gesture. 'I did consult you,' he said. 'You made your wishes in the matter quite clear. What would have been the point in getting embroiled in another futile argument? You've been so against the whole idea of the book that you wouldn't even discuss the subject.'

'I have *never* been against your wanting to write a book!' Diana could hear her voice rising. 'Only against being stuck away on some remote island in the process. You knew how I felt about it, yet you went ahead and made this decision on your own.'

'Yes,' he said, 'I did.' He took a step towards her, his arms spread wide. 'Diana, please try to understand. I *can't* go back. It's simply not possible for me. If anything, these past few weeks of getting back into the social routine have only confirmed my conviction that it's not for me. If we went to Annapolis, it would only be a repetition of the same dull, boring round, and I'd never get my book finished, I know it.'

'I don't see how you can say that,' she retorted. 'You haven't even tried.'

'I *did* try!' Tony shouted. He was growing angry himself now, and his face was set in a firm stubborn expression. 'I did try,' he repeated in a more controlled tone. 'Enough, at any rate, to convince me that I want no part of that shallow, superficial, utterly trivial way of life.'

'It's *my* life, Tony,' she said coldly. 'It's the only life I know. You used to enjoy it yourself.'

'I'm not the same man I was, Diana, and you'll have to understand that. I can't live that way, not ever again. Life is too precious to fritter away on useless parties and idle chatter. I can't do it.'

'And I can't bury myself on an island,' she cried. 'What would I do? I'd be bored out of my mind!' The very thought of it terrified her.

'Maybe you wouldn't get so bored, Diana,' he said, his voice rising again, 'if you just once thought of someone besides yourself and something besides your silly parties!'

She flinched and backed away as though he had struck her. 'That's not fair,' she breathed. 'I came here in the first place because of you.'

He gazed bleakly at her for a long time, then he sighed deeply. 'Maybe that was a mistake. Maybe we were wrong to try to recapture the past.'

As she heard the words and saw the look of defeat on his face, an icy chill gripped her heart. What was he saying? She had to grip the edge of the dressing-table to stop herself from running to him and throwing herself into his arms. She wanted desperately to hear him tell her he didn't mean it, that everything would be all right.

For one brief moment, the thought flashed through her mind that maybe she should at least try what he wanted, go to the San Juans with him, live his way for a while, consider having a child. Surely he'd get sick of the isolation in time, maybe get it out of his system, and they could return to civilisation again. Maybe she owed him that much, and surely a baby would consolidate the marriage.

Then she remembered her pleasant home in Seattle, her friends, all the familiar places, her family, and her courage failed her. Could she give all that up for this man? She looked at him, still not able to speak. I do love him, she thought, but I don't really know him. He had become a stranger again.

Just then a horn tooted out in front of the house, and the spell was broken. Diana glanced at her watch. It was Janet, come to pick her up for the luncheon.

'I have to go,' she said in a dull voice. 'Won't you change your mind and come with us?'

Tony shook his head slowly from side to side. 'No,' he said quietly, 'I won't change my mind.'

CHAPTER SEVEN

THROUGHOUT the luncheon, Diana sat bored and distracted and largely silent. There were enough people present, all talking at once and well fortified with martinis, so that her withdrawn state went unnoticed.

She picked at her food and toyed with her drink, her mind still firmly fixed on the discussion with Tony. What should she do? What *could* she do? His parting remark to her had been that he wouldn't change his mind, and she knew he was speaking about much more than the luncheon. He meant their way of life, their whole future.

His accusation of her selfishness still stung, too. How could he say that she never thought of anyone besides herself when she had come to Kauai just to be with him, to try to make a go of their marriage? It wasn't fair. And what about him? Wasn't he being selfish to insist on dragging her off to some island hideaway so he could write his book? Why couldn't he write it in a civilised place, like Annapolis? It would be an ideal compromise.

She sighed deeply, so lost in her own tormented thoughts that she didn't realise the sigh was audible until Dan, seated next to her, spoke in a low voice below the chatter of the crowd.

'You're very pensive today, Diana. Is anything wrong.'

She quickly put on her brightest smile and turned to him to assure him that she was fine, when, to her horror, she felt the tears gather in her eyes and slowly trickle down her cheeks.

'Excuse me,' she murmured, and rose hastily to her feet.

She began walking through the hotel dining-room towards the lobby, almost running in her haste to get away. She couldn't let her friends see her tears. In the background the ever-present Hawaiian music thrummed, and she stepped outside with relief, sick of the haunting romantic songs.

Out on the terrace, the only sound was the pounding of the surf, and she stood at the concrete balustrade staring out at the breaking waves through a mist of tears.

Then she heard footsteps behind her and in a moment, Dan was at her side. After one brief glance, she averted her eyes, and they stood there without speaking for a long time. She found his silent presence comforting, and eventually the tears vanished.

'Do you want to talk about it?' he said at last.

Diana gave him a weak smile and shook her head. 'I don't think so, Dan, but thanks.'

'It's Tony, isn't it?'

She only swallowed and nodded once.

Dan leaned one arm along the edge of the balustrade and turned to face her. 'He's changed, hasn't he?' he asked. She nodded again. 'You've just got to give him some time, Diana,' he went on. 'After what he's been through, it's bound to take a while to readjust.'

'And what about me?' she asked in a strangled voice. 'How much am I supposed to bend?'

'I don't know, Diana,' Dan said soberly. 'That's got to be up to you. I guess it depends on how much you care.'

'Oh, I care. I care a lot.' She shook her head sadly. 'But

does he? I just don't know any more.'

'I think,' Dan said carefully, 'that Tony loves you very much. But I also think that his experience has changed him in a fundamental way. I don't know. It's as though those years of being so completely alone, friendless, in constant fear for his very life, have marked him for good. But I also think that might not be such a bad thing. Having come so close to losing it, perhaps he values life more than the rest of us do, takes it more seriously, refuses to waste a minute of it.'

'Perhaps,' she said. 'Whatever it is, it's beyond my comprehension.'

'Well, as I say, give it a little more time.' Then he held her gaze in his for a long moment and said, 'But if you ever do decide it won't work, I'll be there, waiting.'

On the way home in the car, Janet was rather pointedly cheerful, regaling the silent Diana with gossipy chatter and touching on every subject except the one that was on both their minds. Diana said little, but carefully managed to sustain a bright smile, laughing at appropriate places and making brief non-committal comments when they seemed called for.

It wasn't until they had turned into the road that led past the house on the beach that Janet finally said something that really caught Diana's attention.

'What did you say?' she asked.

Janet laughed and glanced her way. 'I didn't think you were listening to me. I said we're leaving on Tuesday.'

Diana gazed blankly ahead. The Madisons on Sunday, now the Pattersons on Tuesday. Soon they would all be gone, all her friends. What would she do without them? The days yawned emptily before her, with Tony shut up in his room writing, Leia taking care of the house and meals, Tomo the garden.

'I'll miss you,' she said bleakly.

Janet gave her another quick look, but remained silent as she turned into the driveway. Then, when she had pulled up in front of the house, she said, 'It looks like you have company.' She gave a little wave of her hand.

Diana snapped out of her trance and jerked her head in that direction. A strange dark car was parked just ahead of Janet's. On the back window was an official U.S. Navy sticker.

'It must be Arne Jacobson,' she murmured. For a moment, hope rose within her. Maybe Tony's commanding officer could accomplish what she couldn't, talk some sense into him, persuade him to take the teaching job at the Naval Academy.

Janet switched off the ignition and turned in her seat to face her. 'Why don't you and Tony come with us?' she asked casually. 'We're taking Navy transport, and I'm sure there's room for two more.'

Why not? Diana asked herself. What was the point of staying any longer in Hawaii? Once again she felt a little jab of hope. There was nothing holding either of them here now. The honeymoon was obviously over, all her friends would be gone, and Tony could have all the privacy he needed to work on his book at the house in Seattle.

Janet put a hand on her arm. 'I think it would do you both a lot of good to get into a more normal way of life,' she said kindly. 'It's time, I think. Don't you?'

'You might be right,' Diana replied slowly. 'I think

we're both getting a little restless.' She smiled at her friend. 'Thanks, Janet.'

Janet gave her a thoughtful look. 'I don't want to interfere, Diana, and I'm not looking for girlish confidences. I like my privacy, and I respect yours. So forgive me if I'm intruding, but I'd like to say just one thing.' She paused, as though unsure whether to proceed.

'Go ahead, Janet,' Diana prompted. 'You couldn't possibly say anything that would offend me.'

Janet took a deep breath, then plunged on. 'All right. I think you're going to have to come to terms with the fact that Tony isn't the same man he was. Oh, he looks the same, even acts the same in some ways, but he's not.'

'No,' Diana agreed, 'I know that.' Dan had said pretty much the same thing.

'But you haven't really accepted it, and it's obvious, to me at least, that it's troubling you.' The older woman hesitated a moment. 'If you're going to make your marriage work, I think you're going to have to do the changing, and that's never easy.'

'But shouldn't marriage be a mutual thing?' Diana asked hotly. 'Why is it always up to the wife to change? That's not fair.'

Janet shrugged. 'Life isn't fair, Diana. Haven't you learned that yet? We can't deal with it the way we'd like it to be, only the way it is. All I'm saying is that you have a choice. Tony has done much more than change, he's grown. Growth is always painful. If you want to keep him, you're going to have to grow with him.'

'You make me sound like a spoiled child!' Diana protested.

'Darling, your mother is one of my oldest friends. I remember when you were born. I watched the way she raised her only child. On the one hand, you were given everything you wanted without having to lift a finger, but on the other, you were rigidly trained to follow a certain set of arbitrary rules. They may have worked well for you in the past, but they simply won't do when you're dealing with a man like Tony. You'll have to learn to be more flexible.'

Diana shook her head. The harsh words had both hurt and confused her. 'I know you mean well, and I'll think about what you said, Janet.' She reached for the door handle. 'But I do agree with one thing. We should go home.'

They said goodbye then, and Diana stood watching as Janet drove slowly through the garden and disappeared from sight. She turned and crossed the covered porch to the front door, eager to broach the subject of their leaving to Tony. It could solve everything.

She set her handbag down in the living-room and started walking towards the back of the house. She didn't have much hope that Arne could change Tony's mind about the Navy, but still, he was an ally and had been kind to her. She'd be glad to see him.

But when she reached the door to the lanai, she could see that their visitor was not Captain Jacobson after all. She stood stock still and stared at the scene that greeted her.

Tony was sitting on the chaise-longue, naked except for brief bathing trunks. Seated beside him, leaning towards him, one hand on his bare broad shoulder, was Anne Scott, the physical therapist from the hospital at Pearl Harbor. Her straight golden hair glinted in the sunlight and hung loose, brushing silkily against his back.

A powerful surge of pure rage rose up in Diana's bloodstream, a red haze distorted her vision, and she had to suppress the sudden, compelling urge to throw herself on the lovely blonde woman, to gouge her fingernails into the smooth tanned skin of her face, and pull out that shimmering hair by the roots.

In the next instant, she regained her composure and walked out through the door, forcing her still-trembling lips into a parody of a smile.

'Well,' she said brightly, 'what a pleasant surprise!' Both heads turned at once to face her, and it was then that she saw the black stethoscope hanging from Anne's neck. 'I hope I'm not intruding.'

'Hello, darling,' Tony said easily. 'You remember Anne Scott, don't you?'

Diana nodded. 'Yes, of course,' she said stiffly. 'Does the Navy make house-calls these days?'

Anne laughed, a low throaty chuckle. 'As a matter of fact, yes. Since the doctors couldn't persuade Tony to fly over to Pearl Harbor for his check-up, they sent me to him. The mountain comes to Mahomet, or something like that.' She glanced fondly at him, then back to Diana. 'The Navy won't release him, you understand, without it.'

Diana longed to ask her how long she'd been there in the house with her husband, but she didn't know quite how to phrase it without sounding like a jealous, suspicious wife. Tony, however, saved her the trouble.

'Anne came right after you left, Diana, and Leia fixed us some lunch.'

It was surely almost four o'clock by now. Leia always left at two. That meant they'd been in the house alone for over two hours.

'I'm trying to persuade her to stay for dinner,' he went on, 'but I'm not having much luck.' He rose to his feet and stood looking down at the blonde, a fond expression in the deep brown eyes. 'Won't you change your mind, Anne? We could all go for a swim first.'

Anne jumped up to stand beside him. 'No, thanks, Tony. I really do have to get back. The plane for Honolulu takes off at six o'clock sharp, and I've got to be on it.'

'Well, a drink, then, at least.' He came over to Diana and leaned down to kiss her lightly on the cheek. 'How about it?'

'Yes, of course,' she said quickly, delighted to hear that Anne would be leaving soon. 'Shall we go inside? The sun will be setting soon, and it gets very warm out here until it does.'

'You two go on in the living-room,' said Tony, as they walked into the house. 'I'll just go and put a shirt on and then make the drinks. Gin and tonic okay for you, Anne?'

She nodded. 'Yes, fine.'

When he was gone, the two women sat down side by side on the long low couch. Diana felt a little awkward to be left alone with her, but Anne sat back, casual and relaxed, and smiled at her.

'Tony has made a remarkable recovery, Mrs Hamilton,' she said pleasantly. 'He's in near-perfect physical condition. There won't be any problem with his release.'

Diana gave her a sharp look. 'I'm not sure I understand what you mean by the term "release".'

'For his discharge from active status, of course,' Anne explained. 'You see, the Navy won't put him on the inactive list until they're sure he's fully recovered.' She shrugged. 'I'm not sure why. It seems to me they'd be more concerned about his health if he were to stay in the Navy.'

Diana listened to her words, what she was saying, but didn't really hear her after that first shocking statement. He'd done it, then, gone ahead and applied for his discharge, probably days ago, even weeks, and hadn't told her.

She felt physically ill. Her head whirled. Anne had stopped talking, and Diana could sense that she was staring at her. She was just about to jump up and run out of the room, when Tony appeared from the kitchen with a tray of drinks in his hands.

'Here we are,' he said, setting the tray down and handing Anne her drink. 'I'm a little out of practice. If it's not okay, just say so.'

During this distraction, Diana recovered herself, at least to the point where she believed she could manage to sit there without making an utter fool of herself. She took a long swallow of her drink, then set it carefully back down on the tray.

Tony was seated in a chair near Anne, and Diana could hear them talking together in low tones. She forced herself to pay attention. She'd be gone soon, she told herself, and then she would have it out with Tony once and for all.

'Don't you agree, Mrs Hamilton?' she heard Anne ask.

Diana gave her a blank look. 'I'm sorry,' she stammered, 'I'm afraid I didn't quite catch that.'

'I was just asking if you didn't agree with me that Tony's book will be a huge success.' She turned back to him, her voice eager. 'I'm especially impressed with the way you manage to weave in your whole philosophy about the horrors of war with your experience in prison,' she went on earnestly. 'Those of us who believe that the best way to keep the peace is through military strength have had to suffer long enough from the pacifists' accusations that we're all warmongers.' She turned to Diana. 'Don't you think he's presented an excellent defence of that position?'

Diana murmured a vague agreement, though she had not the slightest idea what in the world the woman was talking about. Her head had begun to ache horribly, and all her muscles felt stiff, as though her joints were locked together.

I've got to move, she thought wildly. I must get out of here. She rose abruptly to her feet, swaying a little, and struggling for some semblance of equilibrium, mental and physical. All her childhood training and her mother's uncompromising rules came to her rescue, then, like old friends.

She reached for Anne's glass. 'Let me freshen your drink,' she said with a polite, frozen smile. She glanced at her husband. 'Tony? How about you?'

He was staring at her soberly, with an odd look on his face that was almost painful in its brooding intensity. He seemed to be attempting to communicate something to her, but she continued to maintain the cool smile, effectively keeping him at a distance.

Anne jumped up from the couch. 'No more for me, thank you,' she said. 'If I'm going to catch that plane, I've got to get a move on.' She held out a hand to Diana. 'Thank you for the hospitality, Mrs Hamilton. I envy you your new adventure.' She sighed. 'I'd give anything to get off, away from civilisation, like that.'

Another surprise, Diana thought wryly. She was almost getting used to them. What new adventure was she talking about? The world seemed suddenly turned upside down. She had lost her bearings, and felt as though plans were being made, decisions taken, actions accomplished, that she had no control over.

She watched in a daze as Anne went over to Tony and held out both her hands. 'Goodbye, then, Tony,' she said with warm affection. 'The best of luck with your book, your new life. I know it will all work out the way you want it to.'

'I'll walk out to the car with you,' said Tony. He darted one swift glance at Diana, then he and Anne started moving away from her.

When they were gone, she breathed a sigh of relief. One more second of that, she thought, and I'd have started throwing things! As she began mechanically to set the glasses on the tray, all her motions rigid, just like an automaton, the anger simmering just beneath the surface began to rise up in her like a huge red wave.

By the time she carried the drinks tray into the kitchen, she was trembling so hard that the glasses rattled against each other when she set them down. She shut her eyes and took several deep breaths, her hands braced on the kitchen counter, willing herself to be calm.

Dimly, as if from an enormous distance, she heard a car start up outside, then the front door opening and closing, then Tony's footsteps as he came back through the house to the kitchen. She was turned away from him, but she knew he was standing there at the door watching her, waiting for her to say something. Well, he could just wait for ever, she thought. She felt as though she might never be able to speak again.

'Diana,' she heard him say in a low voice. When she didn't reply, he came towards her, his footsteps hollow in the silent room. 'Diana,' he repeated.

He touched her, then, tentatively, lightly, on the shoulder, and that did it. A great calm descended on her. She turned slowly around and crossed her arms in front of her, hugging herself tightly to sustain her shaky control. He was staring at her expectantly, his mouth set in a grim line, his face haunted.

'How could you, Tony?' she said. 'How could you?'

The brown eyes narrowed. 'A decision had to be made,' he said curtly. 'I made it.'

'Without consulting me, of course.' She waved a hand in the air. 'You've resigned your commision from the Navy. You've made your plans, I assume, to go off to the San Juans to write your book.' She could feel her temper rising out of control again, but plunged ahead anyway. 'And I had to hear it from her. What else have you and Anne Scott cooked up between you?' she cried bitterly. 'Is she going with you? Is that it?'

'I *did* consult you!' he shouted at her. 'I told you what I wanted, and you refused even to discuss it.'

She quailed a little before his commanding tone, his own fury. He was standing stiffly, every muscle rigid, glaring at her, his chest heaving.

'What *you* wanted,' she said sullenly. 'It's always been what you wanted. How willing were you to discuss what I wanted?'

'I tried,' he ground out. 'I danced to your tune, went to your silly parties, listened to all the gossip, the trivia, until I couldn't stomach it any more. You won't even give my way a chance.'

'All I want is to go home, just go back to Seattle and try to live a normal life!'

Tony spread his arms wide. 'What good would that do? All we'd be doing is changing the locale, the geography, the battlefield, if you will. The life would be exactly the same. You don't want a marriage, you want a scenario out of some romantic novel. Your idea of a husband is a pet monkey you can trot out and parade around in front of your friends when you happen to need one!'

'And what about you?' Diana was screaming now, out of control, deeply wounded by his unfair accusations. 'All you want is a bed partner—but only when *you* feel like it—and some kind of stupid peasant woman to cook and clean and have your children out in some godforsaken wilderness!'

For a moment, she was certain he was going to strike her. His face was drained of colour, his nostrils pinched, his eyes wild, and his hands were clenched into fists at his sides. She lifted her chin, almost daring him to hit her, but suddenly he seemed to crumple.

'This is absolutely pointless,' he said. All the anger seemed to have drained out of him. He gazed sadly at her. 'I love you, Diana, but I can't sell my soul for you.' He sighed deeply. 'I'm afraid it's just not going to work out. It may even be entirely my fault. It doesn't matter. It's hopeless.'

She began to grow frightened then. It was one thing to hurl accusations back and forth in the heat of anger, to air legitimate grievances, but the tone of finality in his voice sent a cold sliver of sheer terror into her heart.

She stood there uncertainly, watching him as he turned away from her and started slowly walking out of the room. She didn't know what to do. If she gave in, did what he asked, went off to his island with him, she was afraid she would only be postponing the inevitable. She'd be giving up the life she loved and probably, ultimately, all for nothing.

Yet if she didn't, she'd lose him. She knew it. He had said he loved her, but the utter finality in his voice had convinced her that he meant what he said. This was no lovers' quarrel, no marital squabble. Their whole relationship was at stake.

She took a step towards his retreating figure, every instinct telling her that anything would be better than doing without him now that she had found him again. He was as necessary to her as breathing. Life on his terms might be terrible for her, might not even work out in the end at all, but without him, it was simply no life at all.

She opened her mouth, then, to call to him, to tell him she would try it his way, but before his name had formed on her lips, she remembered the way he and Anne Scott had looked at each other, the hours they had spent alone in the house, the intimate knowledge the blonde woman had of Tony's book, when she herself hadn't even known what it was about.

He wouldn't discuss his experiences in prison with *me*, his wife, she thought bitterly, but he'd put it all in a book and freely discussed it with *her*!

She did follow him, then. He was standing at the living-room window, his back to her, his arms at his sides, staring out at the sea. It was still light outside. The sun was quite low on the horizon, the blue sky brilliantly aglow with red and orange and gold. The way his broad shoulders slumped tugged at her heart, and she wanted to go to him, to take him in her arms, cradle the dark head on her breast, kiss the wonderful mouth. But the image of him and Anne Scott together intruded once again, bringing with it a renewed surge of resentment.

'Is Anne going with you to your island retreat, Tony?' she asked in a low bitter tone.

He turned slowly around, his expression unreadable, and stared at her for several seconds without speaking. Then his lip curled in contempt and he gave her a mocking smile.

'If you think that, Diana,' he said in a flat, measured tone, 'you're even more shallow and childish than I thought you were. You know damned well there's never been anything between Anne and me but simple friendship. She's a dedicated professional, a mature woman who knows there's more to life than tea-parties and new dresses and the latest gossip.'

'I see,' said Diana in an even voice. 'In other words, she's all the things you want in a woman. I just thought that since you'd confided all your intimate secrets to her, you must also be planning a future together.' She came closer to him and was pleased to see the way his face fell at her words, delighted that she had penetrated his iron exterior at last. 'Do you discuss your "shallow childish" wife with her, too?' She laughed harshly. 'I suppose you tell her I don't understand you. Isn't that the traditional line for disgruntled husbands looking for sympathy?'

'I've never discussed you or our marriage with a single soul, and you know it,' Tony said, recovering his composure. 'Can you say the same? You've got a hell of a nerve accusing me when you still carry on your close relationship with Dan Armstrong. What about all your cosy little chats with him? Can you honestly tell me that the subject of our problems has never come up between you?'

She was about to defend herself, to tell him he was wrong, even though she knew there was a grain of truth to his accusation, but he cut her off with a frown and an impatient gesture with his hand.

'Let it go, Diana,' he said wearily. 'Just forget it. You should have married Dan when you thought I was dead.' He shook his head sadly. 'I don't want us to hurt each other like this. I told you once that I had only one thing on my mind—survival. I can't make it with you, Diana. We tear each other apart. Please, just let it go.'

He turned, then, and strode away from her, out of the room. She heard him go into his bedroom, heard the door shut firmly behind him. She gazed out at the brilliant sky, the colours deepening now as the sun sank lower beneath the blue sea, as though drowning in it.

She knew there was no point in going after him now, even with promises. He meant what he said. It was hopeless. She would just have to let it go.

The next morning Tony was gone. Some time during the night, he had just quietly slipped away, leaving nothing behind, not even a note. Late last night, after tossing and turning for what seemed like hours, Diana had finally taken a sleeping-pill and hadn't even heard him go.

He must have taken a taxi, she thought dully as she gazed out on the driveway and saw the rental car sitting there. She felt drained, empty, and just a little hung over from the effects of the unaccustomed sleeping-pill.

It was raining, not a sudden tropical downpour that was usual in Hawaii, but a steady, slow drizzle that leaked insistently from a leaden sky. A wave of homesickness swept over her. The weather would be like this in Seattle now, she thought, only without the palm trees, depressing as they swayed under their weight of water. Soon the rhododendrons would be blooming in her front garden at home, their stiff upright trusses more suited to being drenched like this than the sodden hibiscus blossoms that drooped so pathetically out near the driveway.

She went into the kitchen to pour herself another cup of the coffee she had made earlier, before she'd started her search for Tony. His bedroom door had been open, the bed neatly made, all traces of him gone, clothing, toilet articles, shaving gear. She had gone through the whole house carefully looking for a note, but there was nothing.

Each room she went into contained a forceful reminder of their short time together. It had been perfect, she thought sadly, as the hot tears poured down her cheeks. The evening swims in the surf, the pool, the chaise-longue on the lanai, the shower stall in her bathroom, even the couch in the living-room, all brought back painful memories of the lovemaking that had carried her to such heights of passion, made doubly delightful by their sheer spontaneity.

Tony had thrown it all away now, with his high-handed, unilateral decision. The unfairness of his actions, his refusal to consider her point of view, made any hope of reconciliation out of the question.

He's really gone, she thought, standing at the kitchen window gazing out at the dull grey sea. It really was over. She'd lost him twice now, but this time she had the strong feeling that it was even more certain, more final, than death.

She set her cup down carefully on the counter. She knew what she had to do, and once the decision was made, her spirits rose. There were arrangements to be made, action to be taken, packing, flight reservations, and she should call her parents to let them know she would be coming home—alone.

She had lived without him once, she vowed silently as she went to the telephone to make her calls, and she could do it again.

CHAPTER EIGHT

'I DON'T know why in the world you want to redecorate the living-room, Diana,' her mother said. 'It's perfect the way it is.'

'Oh, I don't know,' Diana replied. 'I'm tired of it.'

She had been back in Seattle for a month. It was almost April, and the trees had started to leaf out, the daffodils to bloom, and today a pale sun struggled through a clear patch among the canopy of clouds that hung over the city.

Her mother had looked in on her way home from a luncheon, and they were sitting at the round oak table in the kitchen drinking tea. Out in her small back garden, a brilliant pink camellia bloomed, the waxy dark green leaves shining in the shaft of sunlight.

'Are you all right, Diana?' her mother asked, giving her a sharp look.

'Of course I'm all right. Why do you ask?'

'Ever since you came home from Hawaii, you haven't seemed like your old self. I thought you might have picked up some strange tropical bug. Maybe you should see a doctor.'

Diana had to laugh. 'Oh, Mother, Hawaii's as sanitary and civilised as Seattle! I'm fine, really I am.'

The two women were silent for several moments, drinking their tea, but Diana could sense her mother's troubled gaze settling on her from time to time. She knew her mother, though. If she had something on her mind, eventually she would have to come out with it.

She only hoped they wouldn't get embroiled in an argument about going to the doctor for a check-up. There was nothing wrong with her. She just felt a little restless. She always got this way in the early spring, the end of winter.

'Have you heard from him?' she heard her mother ask quietly.

Diana darted a glance at her, then stared down into her tea. 'If you're talking about Tony,' she replied at last, 'then no, I haven't.' She shrugged and picked up her cup. 'But I didn't really expect I would. He made it pretty clear by his abrupt departure that there wouldn't be any communication between us.'

She had never really discussed the subject of their separation with her parents. In fact, everyone she knew had assiduously avoided the whole thing, as though they were all in a conspiracy to pretend it had never happened. In a way, she thought now, it hadn't.

There had been times during the month she had been home, however, when she would have welcomed a chance to discuss her marriage with someone, as though that might bring back the real joys of the short ill-fated affair, convince her that it had been real, that she actually had felt the powerful love and desire that now were fading into a dim memory.

Then she would tell herself that it was better not to discuss it, not to rake up the past, and she would bury the impulse with another distraction. There had been plenty of those, at any rate. As soon as she'd got settled in her house again, the telephone had started ringing, the invitations had come in, and she had resumed her old life as though her recent adventure had been a dream.

Sometimes she even believed it, that Tony had never been released from prison, that he was still dead, that she had never gone to Hawaii, never lived those few short months as his wife.

'What are you going to do?' her mother was asking her now.

'About what?' asked Diana, snapping out of her solitary musings at the sound of her mother's voice.

'About Tony, of course,' was the impatient reply. 'Is there a chance you might reconcile?'

'No, I don't think so,' Diana said slowly. 'I don't even know where he is.'

'He's taken a house on Lopez Island.'

Diana's eyes widened. 'How do you know that?'

Her mother waved a hand in the air. 'Oh, you know the Navy. Everyone knows everybody's business.' She paused for a moment, then went on, 'Anyway, I think it's time you took some action.'

'What action?' Diana's mind wasn't really on the conversation. All she could think of was that he'd actually done it, actually gone ahead and found his place up in the San Juans and moved into it. She knew then, by the sudden leaden weight on her heart, that all along she had still unconsciously nursed the hope that he would change his mind, take the teaching job at Annapolis, surprise her with it, send for her.

Now, with the shattering of that faint hope, she had to face the fact of his loss all over again, and she didn't see how she was going to bear it.

'Well, darling, you've got to do something,' came her mother's sharp voice. 'If there's no chance of reconciliation, then I think you should be free of him for good.'

Diana stared. 'You mean divorce him?' Somehow the idea appalled her.

'I know, dear, it's awful, but what choice do you have? After all, If Tony has seen fit to abandon his responsibilities towards you, you might as well divorce him. He certainly isn't acting much like a husband. Your father and Arne Jacobson are very disappointed in him.' She made a clucking noise with her tongue. 'Resigning his commission, turning down that wonderful offer at the Naval Academy, after all the trouble they went to to get it for him!'

'I suppose you're right,' sighed Diana. She had a sudden urge to defend him, though, and added, 'He did ask me to go with him, you know.'

Her mother gave a delicate, ladylike snort. 'That doesn't sound like much of an offer! You'd be miserable stuck up there all alone, away from all your friends. What in the world did he expect you to do with yourself while he wrote his silly book?'

'Well, he did think we might start a family,' Diana said weakly.

'I think that would be a big mistake, Diana.' Her mother's voice was firm. 'It's much too soon, and Tony is much too unstable to consider such a drastic action. And even if you agreed, you certainly wouldn't want more than one—two at the most. Children are a great deal of trouble, Diana, take my word for it.'

'I suppose you're right,' Diana murmured.

Her mother drained her tea, set her cup down and rose to her feet. 'I'd better be on my way. The Camerons' party is tonight, and you know your father likes to be prompt.' They started walking towards the front of the house, through the spotless kitchen, the perfect living-room. 'You'll be going, too, I take it?' she asked when they reached the front door.

'I suppose so.'

'Is Dan picking you up?'

'Yes, around seven.'

Her mother eyed her sharply. 'You know, dear, if you were legally free of Tony, I feel certain you could marry Dan. He's far more suitable for you—a real gentleman. He wouldn't make any of these unreasonable demands on you the way Tony has.'

'But I don't love Dan, Mother.'

'Oh, love!' her mother said scornfully. 'There's more to marriage than love, Diana. Forget love.'

After her mother had gone, Diana went back to the kitchen to clear away the tea things. The conversation had disturbed her. Ever since she'd come back from Hawaii, she had pushed all thoughts of Tony out of her mind, as the sensible thing to do. It hadn't even been that difficult. After all, she had had seven years without him and only those few short months with him.

That last day on Kauai, when she had to accept the fact that he had really gone, she had made the decision that there was no point crying for something she couldn't have. The ache would always be there, she knew, like a cold little lump of ice in her heart, but if she didn't allow herself to dwell on it, eventually it would lessen, perhaps, in time, even melt away entirely. He had left her, after all. He didn't want her.

She stood at the kitchen window and stared out at the darkening sky. The clouds were growing blacker and closing in. Soon it would start to rain again. She thought about going out in the garden to cut a branch or two of the pink camellia for the living-room, but couldn't quite work up the energy or enthusiasm for even that small task.

What she couldn't forget was that Tony had said he loved her, even that last awful evening in the midst of a bitter quarrel. Then why did he leave her? Why didn't he stay and try to work it out? 'Let it go,' he had said, and she would never forget the look of weary resignation in the haunted brown eyes or the painful droop to the beautiful mouth. It dawned on her then for the first time that he had been hurting as badly as she was.

Was her mother right? Was it better to forget love? The tears stung her eyes as she remembered the perfection of those days on Kauai with Tony. She could just visualise him once again as he came jogging towards her from the beach in his graceful, loping stride, his muscular body tanned and strong, his dark eyes alight with pleasure at the sight of her waiting for him on the lanai. He would gather her in his arms, then, and kiss her, his skin warm against hers and slightly damp from his exertions.

She remembered, too, his comments about the permanency and sanctity of marriage. Were they only hollow platitudes with no real substance behind them, or born of deep conviction? Tony was a serious man. He wouldn't have said such things unless he meant them. But then once again she had to ask herself, why had he left her?

'No!' she cried aloud. The word echoed in the silent house.

I must not allow myself to do that again, she thought sternly. She wiped her eyes with the back of her hand and turned from the window. As she marched purposefully up the stairs to get ready for the Camerons' party, she decided her mother was right. She had to take some action. Until she was free of Tony legally, he would still have a hold on her heart.

Later that evening, Dan and Diana sat across from each other at the oyster bar overlooking the waters of Puget Sound. They were due at the Camerons' at eight o'clock, and he had picked her up, as planned, at seven so they could stop for a quick bite to eat on the way.

Diana was gazing out of the window at the ferry on its way across the bay to Vashon Island, still deep in thought and idly sipping her glass of wine while they waited for their order to be served.

'Penny for them,' Dan said lightly.

She looked at him and smiled. 'Sorry, Dan, I guess I wasn't paying attention. Were you saying something?'

'Nothing important. You're very quiet this evening.'

Diana set her glass down on the table and stared down at it as she turned it around and around in slow circles. 'I've just about made up my mind to divorce Tony,' she said at last.

She raised her eyes from the glass. Dan was staring at her, his blue eyes narrowed, his whole posture tense. He took a swallow of his martini and leaned back in his chair, his gaze firmly fixed on her in a rather severe expression.

'I see,' he said at last in an even tone. 'What brought that on?'

Diana shrugged. 'I had a talk with my mother today. She seems to think it's time I did something about the situation.' She leaned forward slightly over the table. 'Dan, tell me the truth. Did you know he was living up on Lopez Island?'

He sucked in a deep breath and exhaled it slowly. 'Yes,' he said, 'I did.'

She laughed drily. 'Apparently everybody knew—except me. Have you seen him or talked to him?'

'No. I don't think anyone has.'

'Is he alone?'

'As far as I know. From what I can gather, he's doing exactly what he said he wanted to do—get out of the Navy, go off all alone somewhere quiet and write his book.' Dan shook his head slowly from side to side. 'I've got to say I admire his nerve. He's got the whole Navy furious at him, including your father.'

'And do you also admire the way he left his wife?' Diana demanded bitterly. Men! she thought. They always stick together.

Dan gazed thoughtfully at her for a long time, then said, 'I think he's a damn fool for doing that.'

Her gaze faltered, and she turned to look out of the window again. She could still have Dan, she realised, just as he'd promised her. But was that what she wanted? He would be a good husband. He was rather handsome, in a sandy, shaggy way, she thought, turning back to him. Maybe her mother was right and there was more to marriage than love.

'I'm being transferred,' he said quietly.

Her eyes widened. 'When?'

'In a few months. The date isn't firm yet.'

'Where to?'

'Paris.'

Paris! How she would love to spend a year or two in Paris! She searched her mind and came up with the names of at least four couples she knew well who were already stationed there.

'I'd like to have you come with me, Diana,' he went on in a low intimate voice. 'As my wife.' He reached across the table and took one of her hands in his. 'I wouldn't have said anything if you hadn't mentioned the possibility of divorce. You know that, don't you? Tony's my friend.'

'Of course I know that,' she replied.

Just then the waiter came to the table with their order, and while he was serving them, Diana thought over Dan's proposal. Although she had an idea it would be the last time he would make it, she still couldn't quite bring herself to accept it.

Am I crazy? she wondered as she watched the waiter set down the plates of fresh oysters, the crusty French bread, the small bowls of salad. Why am I hanging on to a marriage that is so obviously over? Yet it was more than that, she decided. It wasn't so much that she was clinging to the dead marriage with Tony, as that she wasn't completely sure she wanted marriage with Dan.

She liked him so much, she thought once again, gazing at his kind face, his strong reassuring presence, and she would miss him terribly when he left. She was so used to his dependability, his simply being there in her life. His absence from it would create a tremendous void.

When the waiter had gone, Dan looked at her. 'Well, Diana? What do you think?'

'I think I'm tempted, Dan,' she said slowly. His eyes lit up and he reached for her hand again. 'But,' she went on hastily, 'I can't possibly make a decision until I'm free. Surely you can understand that. How can I promise to marry you while I still have a husband?'

His face fell, and he withdrew his hand. 'All right,' he said stiffly. 'I can understand your feelings.' Then his eyes hardened and his voice took on a sterner tone. 'But if you're going to do it, you'd better start right away. Even I won't wait for ever, Diana.'

She nodded soberly. 'You're right,' she agreed. 'I'll see a lawyer next week.'

Diana was stunned at how simple it was to end a marriage legally. None of her close friends had been divorced, and so the subject had never come up before. They didn't even call it a divorce any more, she learned. It was now a "dissolution", a euphemistic term that didn't have quite the sting in it the older one did.

Now, the following Tuesday afternoon, as she walked in a daze out of the lawyer's office, she couldn't believe the ease with which one could shed a mate. Her father had sent her to his own lawyer, a rather jovial elderly man named Lindsay, who had explained the simple procedure to her very carefully.

As she rode down in the lift of his office building after the brief consultation, she thought over what he had told her.

'There are two ways to handle it,' he had told her. 'If you both agree to the dissolution, then you sign the petition jointly. In that case, you can simply send him the papers and have him send them back after he signs. However, I've found it's much more efficient to deliver the papers in person, just as a little added insurance.'

'And what's the other way?'

He'd pursed his lips at that. 'The other way is a little more difficult. If the other party does not agree, or if there is a problem with the property settlement, then you must file as sole petitioner and have the papers served on your husband as respondent by a process-server.' He had eyed her sharply. 'Do you anticipate a problem?'

'No,' she'd said. 'I'm quite sure he'll want the divorce—excuse me, the dissolution—as much as I do.'

'Well then, I'll have the papers typed up from the information you've given me today and send them to you in a few days.' He'd stood up then, indicating that the interview was over. 'And as I mentioned before,' he said, ushering her to the door, 'it will be much better if you take the papers to him in person. That way you'll make sure he really does sign them right away.'

At the door, she had turned to him. 'Then what happens, after the papers are signed?'

He had smiled broadly. 'Then you return them to me, I file them with the Clerk of Court, and in ninety days you put in a token appearance before a judge, just to answer a few questions and swear to the truth of the statements made in the petition. Then you'll be a free woman.'

It was almost too easy, she thought, as she walked through the noisy crowded streets to where she had parked her car. You sign a few papers, answer a few questions, and wait three months, and a marriage is dissolved as though it had never existed.

Driving home on the busy freeway, she pondered Mr Lindsay's advice that she take the papers up to Tony rather than post them. Could she bring herself to do that, to drive up to Lopez Island and face him again? Wouldn't it be better just to send them, even if it wasn't quite as quick or efficient?

On Thursday afternoon, when the petition for dissolution arrived in the mail from Mr Lindsay's office, Diana still hadn't made up her mind whether to send it or take it up in person.

In his brief accompanying letter, the lawyer had advised her to read over the contents of the petition carefully before signing it, and she obediently sat down in the living-room to do so as soon as she'd finished the letter.

It was all so impersonal, she thought, as she scanned each section of the document, so dry and businesslike. Dates of birth, date and place of marriage, description of common property. Nowhere did it even ask for a reason why the marriage was being dissolved. It was like returning a pair of shoes that didn't fit properly after you'd worn them once, and she found it profoundly depressing.

Is that all there is to marriage? she wondered as she let the papers fall from her hands. She thought of their wedding ceremony, an impressive ritual where, in the presence of witnesses and in God's church, she and Tony had promised to love and cherish each other 'for better or worse, for richer or poorer, in sickness and in health', and only death could dissolve the bond between them.

They had been parted by death once, she thought sadly, but had been given a second chance. She glanced down at the petition, lying on the couch beside her, and felt a sudden revulsion at the mere sight of the shabby document. Yet she had no choice.

She knew she had to go through with it, much as the whole procedure repelled her, but what she couldn't do was just stick it in an envelope and send it to him. She owed it to him—and to herself—to see him one last time, to explain to him her reasons for taking such a drastic action.

She got up and walked slowly over to the telephone. He might not even have one, she thought, but it was a place to start. She dialled information, gave the operator Tony's name, and told her the address was on Lopez Island. To her surprise, the operator gave her a number, and she wrote it down carefully before she hung up.

She stood there for a good five minutes debating whether to call him, even lifting the receiver and starting to dial several times, then replacing it before she'd completed the number. The palms of her hands were getting sticky, and her heart was thudding so alarmingly that she doubted if she'd be able to get a word out even if she did go through with it.

Finally, she clamped her jaw shut determinedly and lifted the receiver once more. This time she finished dialling. She listened to it ring, five, six, seven times, until, with something like relief, she started to hang up.

Then she heard his voice. 'Hello.' She couldn't speak. 'Hello,' he said again, a little impatiently.

She put her hand over the mouthpiece and cleared her throat. 'Tony, this is Diana.'

There was dead silence on the line for a good ten seconds. Then, at last, 'How are you, Diana?' he asked quietly.

'Quite well,' she replied in her brightest voice. 'Busy, as always. How about you?'

'I'm all right.'

Another awkward silence threatened, and Diana didn't know how long she could keep up the trivial conversation. She decided to plunge ahead, and took a deep breath.

'Tony, I've decided to file for divorce.'

'I see.'

When she realised that was all he was going to say, she gripped the telephone harder, slippery now under her damp palm, and hurried on, speaking fast so that he wouldn't notice the shakiness in her voice.

'Since I was quite certain you wouldn't have any objections, my lawyer tells me that all I have to do is get your signature on the petition and he can file it right away.' She laughed nervously. 'It only takes three months, and is a very simple procedure. They make it so painless these days, it's no wonder there are so many divorces! Oh, excuse me, they're not called divorces any more. They're dissolutions now.' She laughed again, a little alarmed at the rising note of hysteria in her voice. She knew she was babbling, but somehow, she thought, if she kept talking, she could hold herself together better. 'No one gets accused of anything,' she went on. 'It's no one's fault, just as though . . .'

'Diana,' his firm voice interrupted her brittle line of prattle, 'I know the process. Just tell me what you want me to do.'

He knows the process, she repeated to herself. He'd been 'dead' for seven years. How did he know the drastic changes in the divorce laws unless he'd researched it himself? She felt suddenly numb, and very cold.

'I see you're already up on the mechanics,' she said stiffly.

She heard him sigh. 'Just tell me what you want me to do,' he said again patiently.

Diana began to grow a little irritated with his tone. He made it sound as though she were forcing the issue and he was simply an innocent bystander.

'It's not entirely a question of what I want, is it, Tony?' she said sharply. 'Don't forget, you left me.'

'Did I, Diana?' he asked. 'Did I really? Were you there for me to leave?'

His gently accusing tone only made her angrier. She opened her mouth to tell him that yes, of course she was there, if he'd only taken the trouble to look for her, but she realised just in time that such accusations and counter-accusations were pointless now. He hadn't changed. Why keep on arguing over an issue that had no more meaning to either one of them? With an effort, she fought down her anger and went on in a calmer tone.

'Since I take it you have no objection to the dissolution,' she said, 'we might as well get it over with as quickly as possible. All it requires is your signature on the petition. Mr Lindsay, my lawyer, tells me it's best that I bring the papers to you in person rather than send them, so the reason I'm calling is to ask if it would be convenient for me to drive up in the next day or two.'

Tony didn't say anything for several moments, and she felt her temper rising again. She hated being put on the defensive like this, and was just about to tell him she'd post the damn papers if it was such a momentous problem for him, when he spoke.

'It sounds as though you're in a bit of a rush. Have you and Dan set a date yet?'

For the first time Diana was aware of a trace of bitterness in his voice, and, to her amazement, instead of the implicit accusation annoying her, it gave her spirits an odd little lift. Somehow it made her feel that she still had some hold on him, if what she did mattered to him.

'I have no plans beyond ending this charade of a marriage,' she said briskly.

'Sorry,' he muttered. 'That was unfair. Tomorrow isn't good for me. How about the day after, Saturday?

Would that be convenient for you?'

Why wasn't tomorrow convenient? she wondered irritably. She didn't relish the thought of driving up north and taking the ferry over to the islands in the busy weekend traffic. He acted as though he didn't want her there at all.

'I don't want to intrude on your beloved privacy,' she said sarcastically. 'You can meet me at the dock if you like, and we can get the papers signed there. If we hurry, I might not even have to wait for the next ferry.'

For the first time, she heard him laugh, a low chuckle deep in his throat. 'No,' he said, his voice serious again, 'I don't want to do it that way. The house is easy to find.'

He gave her the simple directions to his house then, and the ferry schedule, and they agreed that she'd arrive on Saturday about midday.

After they said their terse goodbyes and she'd hung up the telephone, Diana marched straight into the kitchen, poured herself a glass of sherry and drank it down in three swallows. She rinsed the glass out and leaned forward over the sink, resting her forehead against the smooth polished wood of the cabinet door.

What an ordeal! she thought. She felt drained, emotionally, mentally, and physically, and the sherry hadn't helped. She was more convinced than ever that the quicker the marriage was ended, the better off she would be. He still has the power to upset me, she thought bleakly, and I've got to put a stop to it, any way I can.

CHAPTER NINE

DIANA had been to the San Juan Islands often, but she had forgotten how beautiful they were—every bit as lovely as the islands of Hawaii, she thought, viewing them from the top deck of the ferry, only in a very different way. Instead of swaying palm trees, there were stately towering evergreens, Douglas fir, screw pine and cedar. Instead of wide stretches of smooth sandy beach, the coastlines were more rugged, with sheer cliffs plunging straight down into the sea and large outcroppings of boulders jutting out beyond the surf.

It was also colder, she thought, shivering a little in her suede jacket as the brisk breeze blew her dark hair back from her face. Even though the sun was shining directly overhead, there was a distinct chill in the air. She tied a silk Paisley scarf over her head and put her hands in her pockets, then turned her face back into the wind.

It smells so good, she thought, as she drew in a deep breath of the fresh, salt-tanged air. The ferry tooted once as it met its oncoming sister ship, heading towards Anacortes on the mainland, and she could hear the intermittent screeching of the gulls as they wheeled and dipped overhead.

The water here was different from Hawaii, too, she thought, leaning over the railing to gaze down into the churning sea. It even looked cold, varying from a slaty, wintry grey-blue to a brilliant clear aquamarine, depending on the depth of the bottom. Today, because of

154

the wind, there were whitecaps, little foamy ridges that broke the surface of the water as far as she could see.

They were just passing through the narrow channel between Decatur and Blakely Islands. The next stop would be Lopez. From there, the ferry would go on to Orcas, Shaw and San Juan Islands, then to the busy port of Sidney on the enormous mass of Vancouver Island in Canadian waters.

Once they were through the channel, Diana could see Lopez Island just ahead, and she went below to get into her car. In a few minutes she heard the hollow sound of the boat's horn and the clank of chains as the ferry approached the tiny harbour. With a few bumps against the tall wooden pilings on either side, it slid slowly into its berth and the motor was shut off.

Tony's directions were clear and easy to follow. The island was only sparsely populated, mostly by summer homes, and there were so few paved roads that it would be almost impossible to get lost in any case. His house was near Richardson, a small village at the southern tip. From there it was only a mile west on the narrow rutted road that led along the coastline.

As she drove through Richardson and headed west, Diana's heart began to thud in anticipation of the meeting ahead of her, and she momentarily regretted the impulse that had brought her up here. It might have been less efficient to post the papers, she thought ruefully, but it would have been far easier on the nerves.

It will be over soon, though, she told herself as she slowed down to scan the road ahead for the postbox Tony had mentioned as a landmark. I'll just hand him the papers, he'll sign them, and I can leave. The next ferry back to Anacortes was due in an hour. That gave her plenty of time to get her business transacted, but not enough for a social call.

She spotted the postbox then, a gleaming aluminium box set on a rough wooden post. It looked brand new, and had the name Hamilton stencilled on it in clear black letters. Just beyond it was the gravelled road that led to his house, and she turned into it.

Her hands were shaking as she drove around the curving road that snaked slowly downwards towards the sea, and when she got her first glimpse of the house, it was all she could do to stop herself from turning around to go back, to get out of there as fast as she could.

It was a long, low structure built of natural wood and stained a dark brown, and it looked not so much like a human habitation as an integral part of the landscape. Tall evergreens surrounded it, and from a brick chimney at one end, a thin wreath of white smoke wafted gently upwards on the breeze.

What it looked like, Diana realised instantly, was Tony. It was exactly the kind of house she could picture him living in, and the sight of it simply took her breath away. In a single brief moment, a picture of her own house in Seattle flashed into her mind. By comparison, it was like a doll's house, its careful décor somewhat strained and affected, it's neat compact lines artificial.

In the next instant, however, it was gone, pushed hastily away before it could take hold, but the aftershock left her feeling vaguely troubled. By now she had reached a small circular clearing. She turned the car around so that it was facing the way she came, as thought to make sure of a safe getaway, she thought wryly as she turned off the engine and set the hand-brake.

When she got out of the car and turned to the house,

she saw Tony walking towards her, and for a moment her heart simply stopped beating. It fluttered for a moment as he came nearer, then settled down into a sickening, erratic thud.

He looks wonderful, she thought, watching him approach her, tall and straight, the vestiges of his Hawaii tan still on his face. He had on a pair of worn blue jeans and a heavy white fisherman's sweater. He was smiling crookedly, his hands stuffed into the back pockets of his jeans, but as he came closer, she could see the lines of strain in his face, around his eyes and mouth.

He stopped just a few feet away from her and stood looking down at her.

'You're looking very well, Diana,' he said in a rather solemn tone. 'And very beautiful, as always.'

'Thank you,' she said stiffly. The impersonal note in his voice deflated her a little. It was as though he had expressed admiration for a painting or a statue instead of a woman.

'Come inside and see my house,' he invited.

As they walked together down the path, Diana noticed that he very carefully kept some distance away from her so that he wouldn't even brush against her. Was it intentional? But what difference did it make at this point? She reminded herself of why she had come. It was an ending she sought, after all, not a beginning.

They went through a small entrance hall, then into an enormous oblong room with a massive fireplace at one end in which a blazing fire was crackling. The far wall was made of glass and offered a sweeping view of the vast blue waters of the Straits of Juan de Fuca as well as the southerly tip of the nearby larger San Juan Island. The floors were bare polished oak, with colourful Indian rugs scattered about, and the furniture looked massive, solid and very masculine.

Once again she compared it mentally with her own tidy house. She had chosen everything with such care and kept it so immaculate and orderly. In this room there were signs of Tony's occupancy everywhere, from the opened books and magazines lying on the tables to the heavy sheepskin jacket flung casually over an armchair. It was so full of him that she felt vaguely overwhelmed by the impact of his presence.

'Would you like a drink?' he asked politely. 'Coffee? I could make a sandwich if you're hungry.'

'No, thanks,' she said briskly. Somehow it seemed very important to her to get out of this room, this house, and off this island. 'I'd like to catch the next ferry back to Anacortes.' She reached into her handbag and took out the long envelope that contained the typed petition. 'If you'll just sign this, I can be on my way.'

'All right,' he agreed promptly. He reached out a hand and she gave him the envelope. He walked over to the window and started to read, while she watched him nervously. She was very warm, and would have liked to take off her jacket, but she didn't dare.

'It's all very straightforward,' she said after a few minutes. She went to stand beside him. 'As you can see, it's just a simple statement of facts, and all you have to do is sign it there on the back, as joint petitioner.'

Tony gave her a puzzled look. 'I can't sign this,' he said.

Oh, lord, she thought, have I come all this way and gone through all the turmoil of seeing him again just to have him refuse to sign it at the last minute? Along with her annoyance, however, came a little glimmer of satisfaction. Was it possible that he still wanted her?

'Look,' she heard him say, and he pointed at the signature page. 'My signature has to be witnessed and the document sealed by a notary.'

Diana took a quick look. He was right. How could she have missed that? And why hadn't Mr Lindsay pointed it out to her? She hadn't signed it yet herself, so hadn't even noticed that their signatures had to be notarised.

'I don't believe this,' she said, helplessly, looking up at him. 'I've come all this way for nothing.'

She felt like screaming. Her head had begun to throb, and she pressed a hand to her temple. Now she'd have to leave the petition with him anyway and hope he'd send it to her. The whole trip, with all the agonising anxiety about facing him again, had been wasted.

Tony flashed her a broad grin, and her knees turned weak at the sight of it. 'Hardly for nothing,' he said soothingly. 'I have a friend who's a notary. She'll be glad to come over and witness my signature for me. At worst, you'll only miss the next ferry, but another one will be along in a few hours.'

She'd just have to do it, she decided. Two more hours wouldn't make that much difference, and at least she would get the papers signed and in her hands to take back with her. Besides, she felt a sudden spark of interest in meeting Tony's notary 'friend'.

'I guess I don't have much choice,' she shrugged. 'I feel like such a fool for not noticing that.'

'Not at all,' he said. 'It could happen to anyone. I'll just go and make my call.'

The telephone was in the adjacent hall, and she could hear his end of the short conversation quite clearly.

'Jean? This is Tony. I need your professional services

this afternoon.' He listened for a moment, then laughed, a low intimate chuckle. 'No, I have to sign a legal document that needs to be notarised. Why not come for lunch?' There was another pause. 'Good. See you in half an hour.'

'There,' he said, coming back to her, 'that's all taken care of. Now, why don't you take your jacket off, and I'll make lunch.'

As he helped her off with her jacket, Diana noticed that he was still careful not to touch her. Was it indifference? If so, shouldn't she be pleased? He tossed the suede jacket over a chair and eyed her appreciatively.

'That's a wonderful colour on you, Diana.' She was wearing a pair of cranberry-coloured woollen slacks and a matching Shetland sweater. 'Perfect for your colouring.'

Again, his voice was detached, impersonal, and while the brown eyes were warm, she could see no gleam of desire there. Well, she asked herself, wasn't that what she wanted? Not exactly, a little voice answered, and at that moment she didn't know what she wanted.

'Come into the kitchen,' he said, 'and watch my culinary expertise.' She followed him into another large room, bright and sunny, with a red-tiled floor and yellow curtains at the windows.

'Sit down,' he said, indicating a long redwood trestle table in the middle of the room. He began to take things out of the refrigerator, which was painted a cheerful yellow to match the curtains. 'You know,' he called to her, 'this is the first time in my life I've had to take care of myself, and I'm rather enjoying it!' He emerged from the fridge and grinned at her as he carried the food over to the kitchen counter. 'First it was my mother, then the Navy. And, of course, you.'

He turned away then and began to take out utensils and bread from the cupboard. 'How do you like the house?' he asked her over his shoulder.

'It's very nice,' she said. 'It looks just like you.'

'Oh?' He was chopping onions now. 'Is that good or bad?'

'It depends, I guess,' she said evasively, 'on your point of view.'

'I see. Love me, love my house. Is that what you mean?'

'Something like that,' Diana replied vaguely.

'You're welcome to look at the rest of it if you like,' said Tony casually. 'Just wander around, see what you think. Maybe you can give me some decorating pointers. It's not my strong suit.'

It sounded like a wonderful idea. She was growing more uncomfortable by the minute sitting there and watching him work. In fact, she had hardly taken her eyes from him. He looked so tall and strong, she thought, the broad shoulders so wide under the white sweater, the hips so narrow in the worn jeans. He had pushed the sleeves of the sweater up to his elbows, and the tautly muscled forearms, lightly covered with silky black hairs, the large competent hands, brought back a wave of memories she wanted to forget.

'All right,' she said, rising to her feet. 'I think I will.'

There were two bedrooms on the other side of the long narrow main room and down a short hall. One of them was for sleeping, with a large double bed and a connecting bathroom. The other Tony obviously used as a study. The walls of this room were covered from floor to ceiling with shelves of books. His typewriter and several untidy stacks of paper sat on the table in front of the window, and nearby, a straw waste-paper basket was overflowing with crumpled sheets of the same paper.

The more she looked, the more she became imbued with that special ambience that was Tony, and she remembered his earlier statement: 'Love me, love my house.' It was true, she thought, as her eye fell on the dark trousers thrown casually across the bed, the uncapped tube of toothpaste in the bathroom, the towels hung not quite straight. She automatically pulled one off the rack, folded it neatly and put it back.

It's no wonder we couldn't get along, she thought, screwing the cap back on the toothpaste. Yet, underneath, she knew that their respective habits had never been a bone of contention between them. In fact, she had rather enjoyed picking up after him. He was meticulous in his personal habits, after all, just a little absent-minded when it came to the practical, mundane aspects of daily life.

Actually, she had to admit, as she picked up the trousers and hung them on a hanger in the cupboard, this difference had been one of his attractions for her. They complemented each other instead of conflicting. The real problem went far deeper, and had to do with a whole way of life.

She sat down on the edge of the bed and stared out of the window at the rocky beach below. She could never have been happy stuck up here, so far from the city life she loved, much as she genuinely liked the house itself and appreciated the natural beauty of its surroundings.

Yet, on the other hand, the house had definite possibilities. With a little planning, some judicious shopping, what was now a rather stark, bare barn of a place could be transformed into a warm, comfortable home.

She jumped to her feet then and gave herself a little shake. What am I thinking of? she asked herself irritably. I came here to end a marriage, not to move in and redecorate his house!

Just then she heard a car coming down the drive outside, doors slamming, then the sound of voices and footsteps, a loud knocking at the front door. She walked quickly back into the living-room and stood there, uncertain what to do.

'Get that, will you, Diana?' Tony called from the kitchen. 'It'll be Jean.'

With some trepidation, Diana went to the door and opened it to see standing on the other side a tall, fair-haired woman, a rather short balding man and two small children. The woman was carrying a baby in her arms, and when she saw Diana, she gave her a slow, warm smile.

'You must be Diana,' she said, holding out her free hand. 'I'm Jean Nielson, and this is my husband, Warren. Tony told us you were coming today. I'm so happy to meet you at last.'

'Come in,' Diana said weakly, a little overwhelmed by this sudden influx of strange people.

They all trooped into the living-room, and the two children immediately sat down in front of the fire and emptied out the large box of wooden blocks they'd been carrying. Tony strolled in from the kitchen, wiping his hands on a towel and smiling at the newcomers.

'You've met, I see,' he said easily. He turned to Diana. 'The Nielsons are my closest neighbours,' he explained.

'Warren teaches at a school in Friday Harbour, and Jean is a lawyer.'

'A semi-retired lawyer,' the fair woman said with a little laugh. 'At least until this last little Nielson toddles off to school. I am still a licensed notary, however, and at your service,' she added a little bow at Tony.

'Well then, let's get it over with before we eat,' said Tony.

Jean Nielson handed the sleeping baby to her husband, then reached into a capacious leather handbag and pulled out an impressive-looking shiny metal contraption. 'I'm all prepared,' she said, brandishing the seal. 'Let's go!'

Tony led the way over to the table where he had left the petition, followed by Jean and Diana. When he handed it to Jean, she glanced over it briefly, then set it back down on the table. If she had been surprised by the contents, she didn't let on by so much as a word or a look or a flicker of an eyelash.

'Sign right there, Tony,' she said, pointing. 'All I have to do then is sign my own name and seal it.' She turned to Diana. 'I might as well notarise your signature too, while I'm at it.'

It was all over in less than a minute. Diana took the signed and sealed petition and put it back in its envelope. Jean had gone to the children, who were squabbling over the ownership of a particular set of small red blocks, leaving Tony and Diana alone at the table. She wondered what he was feeling at this moment. She herself was filled with an ineffable sadness at the end of their marriage.

She glanced at him. Their eyes met briefly, and he gave her a rueful smile. 'I'm sorry, Diana,' he said softly.

'I wish it had worked out differently.'

The hot tears threatened, and she turned her head quickly away. Without a word she walked over to her handbag, still lying on the couch where she had left it. She put the envelope inside and snapped the bag shut, then glanced at her watch.

As she'd feared, she had indeed missed her ferry. Two hours! she thought in dismay. How am I going to tolerate two more hours in this house with him? She had half decided to leave anyway and wait at the ferry terminal, when she heard Tony's voice.

'Come on, everybody, soup's on!'

Just then there was another loud knock on the door, and a tall, stooped man came bursting inside. His eyes were wild and excited, and his sandy hair stood up on end.

'Sorry to barge in like this,' he shouted at Tony, 'but there's a school of porpoises down in the straits just off the coast, and I knew you wouldn't want to miss it!'

Everyone started shouting at once then, and from then on Diana found herself enveloped in a wave of activity in which she was carried along so naturally that there was no way she could have gracefully extricated herself. The next thing she knew she was walking with the others down the steep path that led to the beach.

'You must be very quiet, children,' she heard Warren Nielson say behind her. 'There's an eagle's nest nearby, and we don't want to disturb them.'

When they arrived down at the shore, several other people were there ahead of them, and Diana hung back a little as they greeted each other excitedly. Then Tony was at her side, taking her hand and leading her towards them.

'This is Diana,' was all he said by way of introduction, and then they all went to the very edge of the shore. Tony put an arm around her and with his other hand pointed out to sea. 'Look, Diana,' he said, his head bent close to hers. 'Do you see them?'

She followed his gaze out over the broad expanse of water until finally she saw them, fuzzily at first, as just an unusually heavy ripple in the near distance, not a hundred yards away. Then, as her eyes focused on the greyish shapes, she saw one leap out of the sea, like a huge sleek fish, until its whole body seemed poised in mid-air. It wriggled for a moment there, then flopped back in the water.

A low cry of delight rose up in unison among the watchers on the shore, as the school of porpoises cavorted and played before them. Except for the breathless oohs and ahs coming from the several children, the low shushes from their parents, and the tide lapping on the rocky beach, there was a great stillness over everything.

Diana stared, transfixed. She had never seen anything quite like it. It looked like hundreds of them out there, the sea full of the graceful creatures, who seemed to be putting on an intricate dance for their benefit, or simply for the sheer joy of it. Some primitive and deeply satisfying emotion filled her being, a purifying, cleansing sensation, where all the trappings and anxieties of civilised life in the world simply melted away.

Then she heard Tony's voice at her ear. 'Wonderful sight, isn't it?'

She turned her head and gazed at him with shining eyes. 'Oh, yes,' she breathed. 'I've never seen anything like it!'

'We even get an occasional whale out there, and a

little farther up the coast, on those large boulders, you can sometimes find seals sunning themselves.'

They all stood there in a line, perhaps twenty people, not counting the children, watching the dancing porpoises, for a long time, when all of a sudden it started to rain. Diana had been so mesmerised by the activity in the water that she hadn't even noticed the sky, which had grown darker by the moment until finally the black clouds opened up in a real torrent.

Everyone turned at once and began rushing up the path away from the beach. Tony put an arm around Diana and held her close to protect her from the worst of the downpour, but by the time they got back up to the house, she was soaked to the skin, her hair hanging dankly around her wet face, her feet squishing in her shoes.

They all stood outside the house under the protective overhanging eaves, stamping their feet and laughing good-naturedly, the children squealing with delight at the unexpected treat.

'Let's all go inside,' called Tony, and after a few demurs about trailing water into his house and his reassurances that it didn't matter, they compromised by taking off their shoes and trooping inside the small entrance hall.

Tony disappeared for a minute, and when he came back he was carrying a large stack of mismatched towels, which he distributed among his waterlogged guests.

'There's plenty of lunch for everyone,' he was saying. 'Warren, maybe you can build up the fire while I see to the food.'

Once again Diana felt as though she were being carried along on a tide she couldn't resist, as the group wandered into the large living-room. For a moment, out in the rain, she had felt a brief spurt of panic at what she'd got herself into, but now the others were so cheerful and seemed to be enjoying themselves so much that there was a festive atmosphere about the whole affair, and she simply allowed herself to roll along with it.

Tony was guiding her towards the fire now, which Warren Nielson had fanned into a roaring blaze. The room was quite warm anyway, obviously heated from another source, and quite cosy, with the fire, the crowd of people filling the room, and the rain slashing against the windowpanes.

'Let's just dry you off, Diana,' said Tony. He put a towel over her head and began rubbing it briskly, then wound it into a turban and put his hands on her shoulders. He gave her a worried look. 'I'm sorry about this. Do you want some dry clothes to put on?'

She shook her head. 'No. Just give me a few minutes in front of the fire.'

She was still a little dazed by all the confusion. The five or six children were sitting on the rug in front of the fire already busy with the blocks the Nielsons had brought earlier, and the adults had broken up into several smaller groups. Someone had turned on the radio, and a lively bluegrass tune filled the room.

Tony went into the kitchen, then, and Diana stood with her back to the fire watching the scene before her and listening to snatches of conversation, all of which seemed to be very animated, even contentious, yet with an underlying note of jovial goodwill.

'For God's sake, Caroline,' a man said, 'turn off that awful twanging and find some decent music on that thing!'

It was the tall, sandy-haired man who had burst in with the announcement about the porpoises, and he was speaking to a middle-aged, rather stout woman.

'Henry,' she retorted placidly, 'don't be such a snob. If I could put up with six hours of Wagner last night, you can put up with a little bluegrass!'

Jean Nielson had come to stand next to Diana, her sleeping baby in her arms. She smiled and said, 'That's Henry and Caroline Decker. He's our local doctor, and she's a painter. Don't pay any attention to them. They've been having this same argument for as long as I can remember and are actually devoted to each other.'

Diana turned to the tall fair woman at her side. 'How long have you lived here, then?'

'Let's see, getting on for ten years. We came just before our first was born. Warren was teaching at the University in Berkeley, and I was practising law in San Fransisco. We lived somewhere about halfway in between.' She laughed. 'We hardly ever saw each other!'

'What made you decide to move up here?' asked Diana, curious why such a capable intelligent career woman would want to leave an obviously exciting life.

'We'd come up here one summer on a vacation and fell in love with it,' Jean explained. 'When I found out I was pregnant, we just decided it would be an ideal place to raise a family, and we've been here ever since.'

'But don't you miss it, the city, the excitement, your career?'

Jean gave her a look that was kind, but tinged with amusement. 'This isn't exactly Siberia,' she said. 'And we aren't in prison. There's plenty of excitement right here, and lots of interesting things to do, if you look for them. For example, Henry Decker and I play together in a chamber music group along with George Thompson and several other amateur musicians.' She pointed at a tall muscular blond man who looked like a football player. 'There's George. He's the only mechanic on the island and takes care of all our cars.' She turned back to Diana. 'Besides, we manage to get into Seattle quite often. The Deckers are just back from Rome, as a matter of fact, and Warren and I are planning a trip to New York later this spring.'

Diana didn't say anything. Apparently this life suited Jean Nielson and all the others, and she didn't want to argue about it. They all seemed friendly, and Tony certainly fitted right in, but she still felt like an outsider, as though she were a spectator watching them, but not really a part of them.

'What do you think of Tony's house?' Jean asked her after a short silence.

'I like it very much,' she replied, 'although . . .' She broke off, not wanting to offend.

Jean smiled at her. 'Come on,' she prompted. 'I won't tell. Although . . . what?'

Diana shrugged. 'It's a little—well, rough,' she said carefully. 'Unfinished, maybe, is a better word.'

'I see. Tony tells me you're a whiz at decorating.' Jean laughed easily. 'I'm a perfect klutz at it, and Warren is colour-blind. Tell me, what would you do for example, to this room?'

Diana knew she was only making polite conversation, but since she was stuck here until she dried off a little, she might as well pass the time discussing her favourite subject. She was also flattered that Tony had mentioned her one talent. It had never occurred to her that he had even noticed. She gave the room a sweeping glance, taking in the proportions, the lighting, the large window wall.

'Well, first of all I'd get rid of those awful rugs,' she said. 'It's a beautiful floor, but it needs refinishing. Then I'd concentrate on a colour-scheme, probably warm rusts and golds with touches of bright olive-green. The walls need pictures, of course, and all the furniture could be re-upholstered in the same natural colours.'

As she spoke, warming to the subject, the room suddenly became transformed, and she could see in her mind's eye exactly what it could become with only a little time, money and care. When she was through, she shrugged diffidently, a little embarrassed by her outburst of enthusiasm.

'Wow!' said Jean with real admiration in her voice. 'I wish you'd come and do my place. We could use a good decorator around here. Everyone else seems to be too busy painting or practising medicine or writing books. And raising children,' she added with a smile.

Just then Tony appeared at the door to the kitchen. 'Let's eat!' he called, and they all started drifting after him, still carrying on their conversations and/or good-natured arguments, whichever the case might be.

It wasn't until everybody else had left, much later, that Diana thought to look at her watch, and when she did, she couldn't believe her eyes. It was past nine o'clock. She'd just have time to get back up to the northern end of the island to catch the last ferry.

Where had the time gone? she wondered. They'd spent over an hour on the beach watching the porpoises, then another two or three hours eating. After that they became involved in a hilarious game of charades. Then

Tony had made coffee, which led to more conversation.

Now, the last of the visitors had gone, and she could hear Tony out in front saying goodbye. In a moment he would be back and they would be alone in the house. Feeling a little uneasy at the thought, she went quickly over to the couch to retrieve her jacket and handbag, still lying there where she had left them when she first came.

When she heard the door shut and saw Tony appear, she started to slip on her jacket, fumbling a little with the sleeves in her haste, and he came to her to help her with it. She had hardly spoken to him all afternoon. He'd moved easily from one group to another, dispensing his hospitality casually, totally at home in the close-knit group. Now that they were alone, she felt suddenly shy of him and anxious to leave.

'You're not going, are you?' he asked.

She picked up her handbag and turned to face him. 'I must. I can just catch the last ferry if I leave now. I should have left hours ago.'

'I don't like your driving home alone at night,' he said, frowning down at her. 'It's a long way from Anacortes to Seattle. It'll be after midnight before you get home. Why don't you stay here?'

She stared at him. 'Stay here? With you?'

He nodded. 'Why not? We are still married, after all,' he said drily. 'You can have my room, and I'll sleep on the daybed in the study.'

Diana was tempted. The room was very quiet now, with all the people gone and only the low fire crackling and sizzling on the hearth. She looked up at Tony. The expression on his face was calm, unreadable, but there was a familiar glint in his deep brown eyes, which she recognised instantly as desire.

She suddenly felt very warm. They were standing less than a foot apart, not touching, but the electric tension between them was working almost like a magnet. She felt herself being pulled towards him, compelled by a force she found virtually irresistible. She stared at the beautiful mouth, the finely sculptured line of his upper lip, the sensuous fullness of the lower.

'Please stay, Diana,' he said in a low husky voice. 'I want you to stay.'

As he bent his head down towards her, she closed her eyes, felt his mouth brush softly against her own. Her heart was pounding, her mind racing. I still love him, she thought in dismay. I still want him.

He was reaching out for her now. She jerked her head back and stared up into his eyes. 'No!' she said in a strangled voice. Then she heard her voice rising almost out of control. 'No!' she cried.

She whirled around and ran out of the room, through the front door. She heard him call her name once, but she slammed the door shut behind her and scrambled up the path to her car without looking back once.

CHAPTER TEN

DIANA never knew how she managed to drive the ten or so miles from Tony's house to the ferry terminal. Blinded by hot tears, on an unfamiliar, badly metalled road, in the pitch dark with no landmarks, she had been impelled and guided by a force fuelled with her panic to get away from that tempting mouth, those soothing arms.

She didn't attain a semblance of calm until she was safely parked in the waiting line of cars at the dock. It was light here. There were other people. She could hear them and see them, and at last her wild pulse-rate began to settle down. She could catch her breath now, and she slumped back in her seat with a sigh of relief, as though she had just escaped a terrible danger.

She glanced at her watch. She had plenty of time, a good twenty minutes. Laying her head back on the seat and closing her eyes, she felt safe at last. Then she wondered, safe from what? She almost had to smile. Tony was no threat to her. He hadn't tried to force her to stay.

In fact, she thought, sitting up straighter, he'd signed the petition quite willingly. His eyes hadn't followed her soulfully throughout the afternoon. There had been no touching, no attempt to get her alone. He hadn't made one overt approach all day, in fact.

It wasn't until she'd been about to leave that his manner towards her had become more than casually friendly. Why had that frightened her so? She thought about the fleeting moment when his lips had touched hers and the sudden realisation that she still loved him. She knew then that it wasn't Tony she was afraid of, but herself and her own treacherous emotions.

And that was why she had to leave, she told herself firmly, get out now before she found herself back on that same old merry-go-round with him, involved in the same old conflicts that led nowhere.

Yet she had enjoyed herself today. It had been strange, but not unpleasant. Perhaps she had been wrong not to give it a try. No, she thought; it was too late. Tony probably didn't even want her any more. He had his new life, his new friends. He didn't need her. He had asked her to stay the night, but only because he was concerned for her safety. Tomorrow he would have been glad to see her leave.

A shrill blast broke the evening stillness, and in the distance she could see the lights of the oncoming ferry. The attendant was approaching her car now to collect the fare. She rolled down the window and reached for her handbag, lying on the seat beside her. When the man bent over to speak to her through the open window, she opened the bag and took out the money from her wallet. He thanked her, handed her a ticket, then moved on to the car behind her.

Diana put her wallet back in her bag and was just about to snap it shut, when it dawned on her that the long envelope containing the signed petition was missing. She switched on the dome light and made a more thorough search, but it simply was not inside her bag where she knew she'd put it.

She went through her jacket pockets then, reached under the seat, the floor mat, went through her bag again, but it just wasn't anywhere in the car. The ferry was bumping against the pilings now, and the other passengers were starting the engines of their cars.

What am I going to do? she thought in a panic. She tried to calm herself so she could think. Could one of the children have taken it? Could she have dropped it on the path in her rush to get away from the house? It didn't really matter. What mattered was that it was gone, and she had to decide what to do about it.

She considered her options. She could get on the ferry, go on home and hope Tony would post it to her. Or she could go back to the house to get it and spend the night. Either way presented a problem. She simply couldn't decide. Her mind wouldn't function.

The debarking cars started coming slowly down the ramp of the ferry. In a minute her line would start to move. She had to make her decision now. It wasn't until the car ahead of her started inching forward, however, and a horn honked impatiently behind her, that she knew what she had to do.

She started the engine, then turned the wheel sharply and veered out of the line, heading back the way she'd come. Calmer now that she had made up her mind, she started once again down the road that cut through the centre of the island. She'd come up here today to get those papers signed, she thought, and she wasn't going to leave without them. One way or another, this thing with Tony was going to be settled once and for all. Tonight.

He was standing at the door waiting for her when she parked in the small clearing and got out of the car. Somehow she knew he would be, and as she walked towards him, she was also filled with the sudden suspicion that at some point in the afternoon he had removed the envelope from her bag himself. It hadn't just vanished all by itself, and she clearly remembered putting it inside just after they'd signed it.

Her step slowed as she came closer to him. He was watching her silently. There was a dim light burning in the entrance hall behind him, outlining his tall lean figure and casting a shadow on his face so that she couldn't make out his expression.

'The papers,' she said weakly. 'I don't have them.'

She was close enough to him now to see him lift an enquiring eyebrow, but his face was grave, the mouth set in a tense line. He seemed to be holding himself very still, every muscle taut.

'I know,' he said quietly.

'You!' she cried in a low voice. 'You *did* take them!'

'Come inside,' said Tony, holding the door open. 'It's cold out here.'

Numbly, Diana went into the house. The fire had burned low by now to a smouldering red glow. On the table in front of it, by the couch, was a bottle of wine and a half-empty glass, and she had a sudden vision of Tony sitting there all the time she was gone, brooding and staring into the dying fire, waiting for her.

'Sit down,' he said. He went to the wood-basket on the hearth and picked up a log. 'I'll build up the fire.'

She sat and watched him as he stoked the hot coals and threw on the fresh log. There was no other light on in the room, and the sudden burst of yellow flame as the wood caught illuminated his face clearly. He is so beautiful, she thought with a little catch in her throat as the light flickered over the fine features that were so familiar to her.

He turned to her then, his back to the fire, his hands in the pockets of the worn jeans, and stared broodingly down at her through half-shut eyes. She sat rigidly on the edge of the couch as though paralysed, waiting, unable to say a word.

Finally he spoke. 'I was hoping you would come back,' he said in a low harsh voice. 'I took the papers out of your handbag this afternoon.'

'But why?' she asked in a strangled voice.

'Because I thought we needed to talk!' he snapped at her. 'I wasn't going to give up on this marriage until we'd at least had a chance to discuss it, but I could see you were bound and determined to get out of here as fast as you could.'

He came to the couch and sat down beside her. 'We've had a month apart,' he said, leaning towards her. 'I've left you strictly alone. I haven't tried to communicate with you in any way. I wanted us both to have time to think things over, make a decision about the future, to see if we even *had* a future.'

Diana stared ahead at the fire. 'I made my decision,' she said dully.

'Diana, look at me,' came his firm voice. Slowly she turned her head, and he forced her to meet his gaze. 'Tell me you don't love me, Diana,' he said softly.

She opened her mouth, but the words wouldn't come. She couldn't lie to him, not now. With a little cry, she got to her feet and started pacing back and forth in front of the fire, wringing her hands.

Finally, she stopped short and stood looking down at him. 'Love has nothing to do with it,' she cried.

Tony's gaze never faltered. 'But you do love me,' he insisted.

She threw up her hands. 'All right! I admit it—I love you. But that doesn't change anything.' She felt the hot tears sting her eyelids, and a helpless wave of self-pity rose up in her. 'Do you know what it cost me to come to the decision to divorce you, to go to that lawyer, to call you, to bring those papers up here?' She was shouting now, almost out of control. 'I thought you wanted it too,' she sobbed. 'You never called me. You didn't even tell me where you were. I had to hear it from Dan!' Her self-righteous anger made her calmer and she pointed an accusing finger at him. 'And don't forget, Tony, you left me on Kauai.'

Tony didn't say anything at all. He got up, filled the glass on the table from the bottle of wine and handed it to her.

'Drink this,' he said.

'I don't want it,' she replied sullenly. She felt drained of emotion after her outburst.

He set the glass down on the table. 'You see, Diana? This is why I wanted to talk, why I asked you to stay when the others left, why I took the papers.' He put a hand tentatively on her arm. 'Whatever happens, we do need to talk, to get these things out in the open. Then we can decide what's best to do, for both of us. Now, please. Sit down.'

Still she hesitated. She felt vaguely threatened just being here alone with him. His hand tightened on her arm. 'The first ferry in the morning leaves at six o'clock. It's almost eleven now. Surely seven hours isn't too much to ask of your time. After all, I did without you for seven years remember?'

He smiled at her then and pulled her gently towards the couch. He was right, she thought. Her anger was spent and her tears were dry. In their place she could feel a small warm glow of satisfaction.

He still wants me, she realised as she allowed him to seat her. He only stayed away to give us time. She had automatically assumed he had rejected her, cut her out of his life entirely, while all along he had only been waiting.

He sat down beside her. 'Diana, we've been through a hell of a time in the past few months,' he said in a low earnest voice. 'After my release from prison, I was in terrible shape, and I can see now what a shock it must have been for you to discover I was still alive after all those years. Then there was all that glare of publicity, which was rough on both of us. The Navy, the reporters, all seemed to be pushing us towards some goal *they* wanted. I was so wrapped up in my own problems that I didn't even take that into account.'

'You were ill,' she murmured, remembering the gaunt, hollow-eyed man she had seen in the hospital at Pearl Harbor.

Tony nodded. 'Yes, ill. And weak. And not, I'm afraid, thinking very straight. What I tried to make you understand there on Kauai was that prison had changed me so fundamentally that I simply *couldn't* go back to the life you and I had once enjoyed together.

'I see now,' he went on, 'that I wasn't being fair to you. I was wrong to expect you to give up a way of life that satisfied you just because it didn't satisfy me.' He gazed bleakly at her. 'The truth is, Diana, that I wanted to eat my cake and have it too. I wanted to live my own way, but I also wanted you.' He spread his arms wide. 'This past month has taught me that I want you more. I can't do it without you. Quite simply, if I can't have you, nothing else really matters to me.'

Diana stared at him, stunned. 'You mean,' she said slowly, 'that you'll give up your house, your life here, come back to Seattle with me, accept the teaching job at Annapolis?'

He nodded grimly. 'If that's what you want. If that's what it takes to get you back.'

Her spirits began to soar. Everything would be all right now. She would have the familiar comfortable life she wanted *and* the man she loved. She could hardly believe her good fortune. He cared for her that much.

'Oh, Tony!' she breathed, and reached out blindly for him.

His arms came around her, and he held her closely up against him, his hands stroking her hair, her face, brushing away the tears of relief and joy that ran down her cheeks.

'God, I've missed you, darling,' he murmured in her ear. 'I was so afraid I'd lost you.' He held her face in his hands and gazed deeply down into her eyes. 'I love you so much, more than my life.'

His mouth came down hungrily on hers then in a demanding, open-mouthed kiss. Diana responded immediately, clutching at him frantically, sliding her hands up under the heavy white sweater to run them over the smooth skin of his back. He pulled away from her to slip the suede jacket off her shoulders, then reached out to touch her breasts, straining tautly now under the thin red sweater. She closed her eyes and let her head fall back as his grasp tightened, kneading the soft fullness. He drew her roughly to him and kissed her again.

Still clinging together, they slid slowly down on to the rug in front of the fire. 'I want to look at you,' Tony said softly, tearing his mouth from hers. He reached out and tugged at the sweater, pulling it over her head, then running his hands down along her upraised arms to her back. He unhooked the wispy bra and slowly drew it off, his hands lingering over her bare breasts.

He tore off his own sweater and leaned back against the couch, settling her up against him between his long legs. His arms came around her from behind, and they lay there quietly for a while, both facing the fire. Then, as his hands began to roam over her body, he buried his face in her hair, murmuring in her ear, telling her how much he loved her and wanted her until she felt choked with desire.

He raised her gently to her feet. 'Let's go to bed, darling,' he said, his eyes never leaving hers. Diana only nodded, and he picked her up and carried her down the hall to the bedroom. He set her down by the side of the bed. Silently, they removed the last vestiges of their clothing, then stood facing each other.

'I'll never stop loving you, Diana,' he said softly. 'I want you with me for ever.'

'I know, darling,' she said. 'It's what I want, too.'

They sank together down on to the bed and lay there wordlessly for several moments, locked in each other's arms, until the tension became to much to bear. With a groan, he rolled towards her and threw himself on top of her, his mouth hot on hers, his hard need pressing into her, his breath coming in short laboured rasps. She shifted her body under his until they were joined together and reached the pinnacle of love once again.

Some time in the early hours of the morning, at dawn's first light, Diana awoke beside her sleeping husband. At first, she felt disorientated in the strange surroundings, and it took a moment for her to get her bearings. She raised her head slightly off the pillow, wide awake now, her eyes scanning the unfamiliar room.

Then Tony stirred in his sleep, and his hand moved up from her waist to settle on her bare breast. She lay back down with a sigh of contentment as memory came flooding back. She put her hand over his, pressing it closer over her heart, and smiled up at the ceiling.

Everything was all right now, she thought happily. Tony would come home with her where he belonged, and they would live happily ever after. In time he would settle back into Navy life again, and the past would be forgotten.

She turned her head carefully to look at him. His face was relaxed in sleep, the dark thick eyelashes resting on his cheekbones, the beautiful mouth slightly open, the black hair tousled. She longed to reach over and smooth it back, but didn't want to disturb him.

Yes, she thought, gazing her fill at the sleeping man, she had her old Tony back again. Then she frowned. No, she amended, not quite the old Tony. She noticed then the fine lines around the corners of his eyes, the few silvery strands among the black hair, the more prominent bones in his face.

She suddenly recalled Janet Patterson's observation that not only had Tony changed, he had grown, and that if she wanted to keep him, she would have to grow with him. Diana was beginning to get a glimmer now of what Janet had meant, and she looked at him again with new eyes. He was no longer a carefree boy. Through his ordeal, he had become a serious man.

She wondered then just how long he would really be

happy trying to fit back into a way of life he had outgrown. In time, would he come to resent the fact that he had given up what he really wanted for her sake?

She thought about her own life then, comparing it with what she had seen yesterday of the people who lived here, the easy camaraderie, the pleasure in simple things, the awesome beauties of nature, children, good company, music, even the silly games. Somehow these all made her own endless round of social affairs, shopping, gossip and idle chatter seem frivolous and trivial.

She remembered, too, her own growing disenchantment with it over the past month. At the time, she had assumed it was merely due to the unresolved situation with Tony, the limbo of their marriage. Now she wasn't so sure.

A sudden icy chill clutched at her heart. Was she a shallow person? She thought about Jean Nielson, apparently so contented and fulfilled with her three children, her law career to return to, and of Caroline Decker, who found her own satisfaction in painting.

These people were not rotting in a stagnant backwater, not by any means. The realisation hit her like a thunderbolt. Far from it, in fact. They travelled to Europe and New York, took weekend trips into the city, played chamber music, yet at the same time remained deeply committed to the solid, substantial life of this beautiful island.

By now her head was whirling in confusion. She gently disengaged Tony's hand from her breast and slid slowly out of bed. He muttered briefly in his sleep, then turned around, burying his head in the pillows.

She found a robe hanging in the cupboard, slipped it on, and padded barefoot down the hall into the living-room. It was growing lighter by the minute, and through the broad expanse of glass, she could see the sun just rising above the horizon to the east, suffusing the surface of the sea with a soft yellow glow.

A gull began to shriek, and she saw it rise up off the rocky beach and dive down towards the water, just at the spot where they had seen the school of porpoises playing yesterday. The tide was just going out, and along the foamy shore she could see what looked like a family of sandpipers waddling along scavenging for food.

She went into the kitchen to make some coffee. While it was perking, she sat down at the redwood table, her chin in her hand, her mind automatically speculating about ways of making the large bare room more attractive. The yellow curtains and tiled floor could stay, she thought, but she'd paper the walls and hang copper utensils over the stove, paint the bare wooden rafters, find a colourful rug ...

She stopped short. What was she thinking of? Then she remembered what Jean Nielson had said about the island needing a good decorator. Was it possible her one small talent could be of value to someone else?

The thought boggled her mind, and she jumped up from the table. For the first time in her life, it occured to her that her existence on this earth might be for some other purpose than just blindly following someone else's rules and having a good time.

Still deep in thought, she poured out two mugs of coffee and took them back into the bedroom. Tony was still asleep, on his back now, his arms at his sides outside the covers, his broad chest bare.

Diana set the coffee down on the nightstand and stood looking down at him. She knew then that she could never force him back into a way of life he would eventually find intolerable. It would be like caging a splendid wild animal, putting him back in the prison he'd just escaped from.

She loved him too much to do that to him. He would do it, probably, bite the bullet and go through with it for her sake, but in the end it would kill the very qualities she admired and loved most about him.

As she gazed at the long lithe body outlined under the blanket, she had a sudden vision of what it would be like to have his children. He had wanted to start a family, and now she knew he was right. What better way to cement the bond between them?

She sat down on the bed and leaned over him, resting her hand on the solid-muscled chest. He blinked once, then opened his eyes and smiled at her, raising himself up slowly on his elbows.

'Good morning, darling,' he said, putting his hand over hers. 'Kiss me.'

She bent down and pecked at the corner of his mouth, then raised her head again, amused at his sudden frown.

'That's not much of a kiss,' he complained, reaching out for her.

'Later,' she promised with a little laugh, pushing him away. 'Right now I want to talk.'

Tony crossed his arms behind his head and leaned back against the pillows. 'That sounds ominous,' he said, narrowing his eyes warily at her. 'But fire away.'

Diana took a deep breath, hesitated a second, then plunged into the icy waters of the unknown. 'I've changed my mind, Tony. I don't want to go back to Seattle, the Navy, Annapolis. I want to stay here.'

He sat up straight then, the blanket falling away

heedlessly, and stared at her. 'Are you serious?'

She nodded happily at the gleam of hope and pleasure that lit up his warm brown eyes. 'Never more serious,' she assured him.

'You'd do that for me?'

'It's no more than you were willing to do for me,' she said softly. 'I love you, Tony. I was wrong to try to change you. I was the one who needed to change.'

She flung herself on him then, clinging to him and nestling against the bare broad chest. His arms came around her, and he sank back on the bed, carrying her with him.

She looked down at him. 'I want to be a real wife to you, Tony,' she said earnestly. 'I want to make a home for you, take care of you, so you can write your books. I want to be part of *your* life now, get to know *your* friends. And,' she added, 'have *your* children.'

He didn't say anything for a long time, but the look of pure love and joy on his face was enough to tell her how happy she'd made him.

'You're sure?' he said at last. She nodded. 'Then give me that kiss you promised me,' he added softly, pulling her head down.

As their lips met and his arms came around her, Diana knew she'd done the right thing, probably the rightest thing she'd ever done before, and that although there might be problems ahead, she'd never regret it. Tony's castle in the air had been built for her too, she saw now, and all she had to do was walk inside.

Harlequin Presents

Coming Next Month

Available in November wherever paperback books are sold, or through
Harlequin Reader Service:

In the U.S.
901 Fuhrmann Blvd.
P.O. Box 1397
Buffalo, N.Y. 14240-1397

In Canada
P.O. Box 603
Fort Erie, Ontario
L2A 5X3

Can you keep a secret?

You can keep this one plus 4 free novels

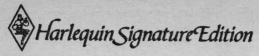

Penny Jordan

Stronger Than Yearning

He was the man of her dreams!

The same dark hair, the same mocking eyes; it was as if the Regency rake of the portrait, the seducer of Jenna's dream, had come to life. Jenna, believing the last of the Deverils dead, was determined to buy the great old Yorkshire Hall—to claim it for her daughter, Lucy, and put to rest some of the painful memories of Lucy's birth. She had no way of knowing that a direct descendant of the black sheep Deveril even existed—or that James Allingham and his own powerful yearnings would disrupt her plan entirely.

Penny Jordan's first Harlequin Signature Edition *Love's Choices* was an outstanding success. Penny Jordan has written more than 40 best-selling titles—more than 4 million copies sold.

Now, be sure to buy her latest bestseller, *Stronger Than Yearning*. Available wherever paperbacks are sold—in October.

Harlequin Intrigue
Adopts a New Cover Story!

**We are proud to present to you
the new Harlequin Intrigue cover design.**

Look for these exciting new stories, which mix a contemporary, sophisticated romance with the surprising twists and turns of a puzzler . . . romance with "something more."

Plus . . . we are also offering you the chance to enter the Intrigue Mystery Weekend Sweepstakes in the October Intrigue titles. Win one of four mysterious and romantic weekends.

Buy the October Harlequin Intrigues!

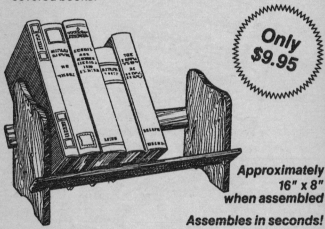